TRACES OF BOOTS ON TONGUE

SEAGULL
BOOKS
•
CELEBRATING
40 YEARS

THE INDIA LIST

RAJKAMAL CHAUDHARY

TRACES OF BOOTS ON TONGUE

and Other Stories

Translated by Saudamini Deo

LONDON NEW YORK CALCUTTA

Seagull Books, 2023

The stories collected in this book were published
in Hindi by Rajkamal Prakashan in 1995 as part of the volume
Pratinidhi Kahaniyan by Rajkamal Chaudhary (1929–1967)

Original Hindi text © Rajkamal Prakashan

First published in English translation by Seagull Books, 2023
English translation © Saudamini Deo, 2023

ISBN 978 1 80309 079 5

British Library Cataloguing-in-Publication Data
A catalogue record for this book is available from the British Library

Typeset by Seagull Books, Calcutta, India
Printed and bound by WordsWorth India, New Delhi, India

CONTENTS

Translator's Introduction

In New Delhi, a young painter is thinking about Henry Moore's *Reclining Figure*. He likes the colour blue and wishes to paint a portrait of a woman whom he thinks he knows. He decides to walk to Man Singh Area from Connaught Place, in the burning afternoon heat. Memories of a filthy experimental art studio. Someone recounts an accident. There is a glass fairy, a painting passed off to another, a promise of Paris. He wants to say something, but the young Delhi painter remains silent.

It's the middle of the twentieth century, a decade or so after India's independence from British colonial rule. The world is still reeling from the aftermath of the Second World War and feeling the effects of the continuing Cold War. The Korean War and the Vietnam War have begun as has the Cuban Revolution. Assassination of John F. Kennedy. Insurgency in Northeast India. Indo-Pakistan War. Sino-Indian War. The Algerian War. India is a new republic, a young socialist country; poverty is rampant, and disenchantment has begun to set in after decades of fervent and passionate political movement. There is an eerie feeling that the present does not quite resemble the once-promised future.

Somewhere in the middle of this, an unnamed narrator, a salesman from Calcutta, is trapped in the dark basement of a brothel in an anonymous town. There are others with him: an indifferent factory engineer, a young student, an old coal supplier with a useless family, at least two prostitutes, many dead rats, a venomous snake, shards of broken glass, stubs of just-extinguished cigarettes. The narrator, visiting the brothel for some quick sex, is overwhelmed by the horror of the basement. The old coal supplier has been bitten by a snake. He cries for help while bleeding to death but no one cares. The brothel basement that is drowned in darkness begins to resemble life itself, from which there is no escape except by death. Life itself is the burning house.

Elsewhere, an unnamed writer, a man in his 30s, is observing objects in his room: the hard cement floor, the inflated mattress bought from an auction house, sheets of newspaper, a closed window frame, a mirror, a sick man standing in front of a mirror. A Siamese cat. He goes out to meet his girlfriend at a restaurant in Connaught Place where he is fixated on the image of a woman in a poster. His mind is blurring the women surrounding him and the woman in the poster. He contemplates life, death and suicide but there is no longer any difference between the bathroom mirror and the mirror in his room. Every object, every person is blurring into another, until it is no longer possible to differentiate between life and death.

This strange, almost absurd ambiance is peculiar to the meaningless world of Rajkamal Chaudhary.

This sick man standing in front of his mirror-vortex could be Rajkamal himself. Chaudhary's quintessential protagonist is a young man, often a proxy for himself, caught in the postmodernist world where nothing seems to have any meaning any more. The young men of Chaudhary's stories are struggling to survive in a newly independent India, where the very idea of a future remains a mirage. There are women too, often regarded from a distance but equally experiencing the horrors of life firsthand: a hysteria patient obsessed with a black cat; a woman who converted to Hinduism searching for her lost Christian past in cemeteries; a young woman living in a village who has just had a strangely terrifying sexual encounter. The characters' realities swing between privileged and unprivileged India, often complicated by financial and social pragmatism, which compels them to eventually resign themselves to the existential ennui they feel in their very bones. They must now get used to the absurd horror that is life.

It is perhaps not an exaggeration to say that Chaudhary was the first rebel or avant-garde writer of Hindi literature, someone uncomfortably uncategorizable, writing outside the given dicta of moralistic Hindi literary movements. A star writer of literary magazines, he was never quite fully accepted into the folds of the Hindi literary mainstream, always considered too vulgar, too immoral, too degraded to be deemed a writer of importance. It is his last poem, however, written on his deathbed, that founded the basis of contemporary modern Hindi poetry. Without Chaudhary's 'Muktiprasang' [Freedom episode], we would not have arrived at Dhoomil, Raghuvir Sahay, not even Alok Dhanwa. Chaudhary was perhaps the first to experiment with the cadence in which Hindi contemporary poetry and prose is being written even today. When he fell ill, Agyeya visited him in Patna. This visit by the iconic writer created a commotion in the literary world of Bihar which until then hadn't quite realized the importance of the strange ailing writer. It was around the same time that Agyeya wrote an existential letter to Rajkamal, parts of which were published at the beginning of his 'Muktiprasang'.

Named Manindra Narayan Chaudhary after his birth in 1929, at Rampur Haveli in northern Bihar, his childhood was marked by a strictly religious upbringing, the early death of his mother and the subsequent tensions with his father who married a much younger woman. It was perhaps in high school in Nawada that he first started writing poetry in Maithili. He then moved to the capital Patna to study in an arts programme, where painting briefly interested him. But, quickly distracted by a love affair, he moved to Bhagalpur where he enrolled in another programme. It was finally in Gaya that he completed his education. He had married his first wife Shashikanta Choudhary by then, and despite an immense dislike for routine, started working for the government at the Patna Secretariat. It was around this time that he decided to also write in Hindi, which promised a wider readership and more money than Maithili.

He was eventually dismissed from his government job on account of a long absence, owing to a complicated relationship with a woman named Savitri Sharma. The relationship lasted about a year-and-a-half, including an eight-month long marriage, which broke down (depending on the source) either after his romantic involvement with his wife's niece, or over an incident involving a platinum ring. He returned to his first wife and moved to Calcutta, where he got involved with numerous women, and came into close contact with the Bengali avant-garde literary movement piloted by the Hungry

Generation. Chaudhary remained in Calcutta for another six years, working both as a translator and a writer (under his own name as well as numerous male and female pseudonyms). In 1960, he founded a literary magazine, *Raagrang* that he continued to publish until 1963 when he returned to Patna. There, he worked as an editor for *Bharat Mail* for some time, after which he devoted his time entirely to his writing. In 1966, he fell ill with suspected lymphosarcoma. He died at the age of 37. By then, he had already written 11 novels, 7 short story collections and hundreds of poems in Maithili and Hindi.

The stories in this collection are montages, flashes, almost documentary-like glimpses of the past that no longer feel like the past. Much like the nouvelle vague cinema that broke down boundaries between reality and fiction, Chaudhary's stories seem to reject the characteristic formality of earlier Hindi literature and embrace a newer, more modern cadence of a world where there is no longer either god or morality, not even the desire for it. He is a writer writing not in a closed room but on the streets, in *plein-air*.

In writing these modern bewildered and bitter characters trying to cope in a society that is fast breaking down, Chaudhary perfectly encapsulates not just the twentieth-century Indian existence but also the twenty-first-century one. In this, it seems that he perfectly encapsulates the twentieth and twenty-first century *earthly* existence. Written more than 70 years ago, the stories sometimes read like they were written just this morning, but, like in life, there are no resolutions on offer and no final meaning to be arrived at.

The characters, like us, must survive without knowing why.

STILL LIFE

I wake up late. I sleep on the floor. Mostly, I do not sleep, I stay awake. An unknown bird fluttering its wings in the black of sleep. How hard is this floor made of stone chips and cement! How needless! There can be no other use for this floor. Not even for writing history.

When I lie down, I start to sink, this spring mattress bought from a large auction house. It is too swollen. When I lie down, it feels like the ground beneath me is sinking. The mattress is printed with Japanese-style flowers. Beautiful and neon, like that nanny from the mountains who once made my father run away with her. When they returned a month later, draped in dirty clothes, looking extinguished, how much my mother had laughed! How elated she had been, running swiftly from here to there, informing the neighbors, calling the priest for the puja. Telephoning my father's friends. I was just a child, yet I thought Ma would now go mad. She would go mad, and Father would send her off to Ranchi's mental hospital. And that nanny from the hills, printed in the Japanese style, would trap me in routine; tea at seven, study till ten, come home from school at three, snacks at four and then home again by six in the evening.

I couldn't do it. I can't do it. I am so tired that I fall asleep immediately. The pages of the newspaper are crushed under my arms. I can't finish reading the newspaper on any night. Ramlal Kahaar raped and murdered his sister, then threw the body under the Bali Bridge. I think I will go to the court tomorrow. The case is ongoing; I want to see what kind of a man this Kahaar is. A simple, decent man or a ten-headed twenty-limbed monster! Sleep arrives. I awake only after the sunlight is bright. Sleep. Sunlight. Sharp light. A crowd running through the streets. Chimneys belching smoke. Sounds. A fat woman bathing near a pipe out in the front. Her crying child. Nationalist songs on the radio—this nation is ours. This earth is ours. On the wall, a girl stilled in a photograph for a long time. My mother. My nanny from the hills. My sister, whom I have murdered and thrown under the Bali Bridge. But not that girl, not that stilled girl.

That girl, who will soon leave her house. She will come to Connaught Place on a scooter. She will look at the pedestrians with disgust. 'Tell me, what has happened to you?' We will meet in some restaurant in Connaught Place, we will sit apart from each other, she will ask questions: 'Tell me, what has happened to you? Why are you becoming like this?' We are sitting apart from each other, today she has tied her hair into a thick bun, like a Bengali woman, and casting her face into thick layers of melancholy, she doesn't want to explain to me why her mother still won't let her take the car. 'Tell me, why didn't you shave today? Tell me. Why didn't you go to the art-theatre people? I had arranged everything. Seven hundred rupees for one play is not bad. Then the book would have been published. You would have got some money from that, too. Who are you taking revenge on?' She kept talking and standing on a small stage, holding a mic, looking.

If I smash this girl's head with the blue bottle of cona coffee, under which Act of the Indian Penal Code will I be arrested? Perhaps they won't arrest me, only laugh at my stupidity. A girl stilled inside a photo frame cannot be injured. Neither from the cona coffee bottle nor from the green bottle of Vat 69. She is not a girl, only a photograph. A girl sitting on the corner of a sofa with her Siamese cat. Nature morte. Still life.

I do not hate this life. I adore it. I love it. I love still life, life broken from the exhaustion of constant movement. This is my destiny. I wake up late. I stand up and straighten my arms. On the right, the closed window frame, also picked up from an auction house.

A sick man in front of a mirror. A man wants to die. Suicide. Long sleep. Sunlight. Sounds. This country of ours. Our earth. A crawling crowd on the streets. Sharp light. On the wall, a girl stilled in a photograph for a long time. A Siamese cat. A sick man. Beginning from suicide and ending at suicide. Life begins from here, and, upon its return, ends here. Meaning, my life. Not anyone else's, only my own. I wake up in the morning, stand in front of a mirror and look at my hands—the blood no longer stains my fingers. Only the scent remains. All the perfumes of Arabia will not sweeten it. I feel scared. I move my face closer to the mirror and, looking at my pupils glowing in colossal abysses, I feel scared. Life begins from this fear. Life ends due to this fear. End. Beginning. There is not even a slight difference between the two. There never was.

There never was, so I have come to Connaught Place. That is why I come. She hangs up the telephone. She hangs up after saying just this: 'The restaurant opens sharp at nine.' That restaurant, where it feels like we are sitting on the chest of a volcano. Lava is oozing out. A ruby fog. And the dark has turned so yellow.

I didn't answer her. I kept drinking each drop of the coffee silently with a spoon. This Anglo-Indian girl on the mic. Waiters moving like white shadows in the yellow darkness laugh at something said by a boy in the corner. I have turned so old and ugly. How ill! Who can keep me from dying? Why would anyone stop me?

'Tell me. Where do you find alcohol so early in the morning? And today is a dry day too.' She shook her shoulders slightly. She has arrived with her hair tied in a big bun, like a Bengali woman. 'Where do you find so many roses for your bun? It's not even the season of flowers.' I want to call her close to me and ask. But I can't. That Anglo-Indian girl is looking at us. Why are all these people sitting away from each other? She starts a song in a faint tune. That dream for which sleep is not necessary. I start laughing. I laugh at this break-up between sleep and dream.

Shirin is surprised. She looks at me angrily. I keep laughing. Then I say, 'I am sick of it. I don't want your art-theatre money. Why don't you try to understand what I am saying? What will I do with money?' I then look at the coagulated anger on Shirin's face. Her mother is some minister's special friend. There is no father. There was perhaps never any father. There was once a wise man who did business with revolutionaries by filling coconut shells with alcohol, opium and gold. That wise man is now a minister. Every evening, Shirin's mother first goes to a ladies' salon, then attends that minister's special court. But the mother's daughter is not that wise. She leaves home at eight in the morning, then waits in this restaurant for a sick man till ten. Why does she wait? Why does she get angry?

Why does she lower her face in melancholy, which Buddhist princess from which Ajanta's fresco does she resemble in that expensive printed Khadi saree? I start feeling furious. I feel furious with myself. Can't a person live without money? Can't they be happy? And happiness is not necessary. Life is necessary. To keep living is necessary. To live anyhow. But is it not possible without money? Must one be sold somehow?

I think she is slowly getting bored. This thirty-year-old melancholy and innocent girl! Thirty years are not few. But Shirin is still wrapped in the books of childhood. She wants dreams, not sleep. Not death. She wants death, but she also wants a Taj Mahal to be built on her grave. Is it not possible? Nothing is possible in this era of democracy. Everything is impossible. Even that which happens. What doesn't exist is also impossible. Socialism. Sunlight. Sharp light. A crawling crowd on the streets. A procession chanting savage slogans. Man. A half-naked fat woman bathing near the pipe out in the front. Nationalist songs on the radio. Shirin doesn't understand that I have a desperate need for money, and that is why I hate it. I need money. For nothing else but for my two–three-year-old daughter whom I have left with my mother. But is it necessary for that girl to be alive?

'Who are you thinking of? If you had to be so silent, you could have just refused. I wouldn't have come. It would have been better to go to the club,' Shirin said. In the thirty-year-old Shirin, I was looking for my thirty-year-old daughter. She will say the same thing when she grows up. Every girl says the same thing to every man. Then, she goes to another man. Doesn't want to be still. Doesn't want to be still like a picture. To be still is also death. And are we not all stilled in this endless extension of time? Does this meandering have any meaning? Any significance? Any other analysis?

There is no analysis because all the old meanings have turned stale. All the meanings are broken. All the analyses are false. 'Go, you can go now. Keep bathing. Until you drown. Keep bathing, Shirin! Until you drown . . . ' I said in a voice so hard and flat that the girl about to begin a second song felt scared. She fell silent. She turned around and started talking about us to the people playing the violin behind her. Then she burst into laughter.

Her free laugh broke Shirin's heart. She was hurt. She didn't say anything. She stood up silently and, without looking at me even once, began to walk out of the restaurant. For some time, I kept staring with morose eyes at the door shimmering in the yellow dark. She left like a dream shattered by a sudden awakening. She paused for a moment near the door. She didn't turn, didn't look at me. She paused silently. Like a statue. Like a stilled image on a wall. Then she opened the door and went out. I get up and go straight to the bathroom. I have a small phial of rectified spirit in my pocket. My liver starts burning. I feel like I will vomit and my intestines will be pulled out with my phlegm. It is dark. An immensely yellow dark. And I am standing in front of the bathroom mirror. This mirror was also bought from an auction house.

A sick man standing in front of a mirror. A Siamese cat. A girl. On the wall, a girl stilled in a photograph for a long time. My mother. My nanny from the mountains. My sister. My little three-year-old daughter. A dream for which sleep is not necessary. A dream for which there is nothing else. This dream is death. It is suicide. Life begins at this suicide and ends at this suicide. At the age of 60, Maupassant's old man remembers the smile of a young girl, that moment's smile when the old man was a young boy. Naive. Unknown. And I am that boy who, in this strange environment, has suddenly turned into an old man of 60. There is no age. Man doesn't have any age.

When I returned from the bathroom, I saw that Shirin had come back and was talking to that same Anglo-Indian girl on the stage. The song is over. There is no one in the restaurant except the waiters. Shirin is blushing. Shirin is blushing while saying something to the singer girl. There is no volcano. Now this restaurant is not a volcano, it's a stilled song.

Shirin is here and is now still inside the picture frame on the wall with her Siamese cat. And now I am awake. I wake up late. I sleep on the floor. Mostly, I do not sleep, I stay awake. An unknown bird fluttering its wings in the black of sleep. How hard is this floor made of stone chips and cement! How needless! There can be no other use for this floor. Not even for writing history.

SOME PEOPLE IN A BURNING HOUSE

There is no place for doubt. That house was a brothel. Not a temple. Not a hotel either. Shamshad had said—You won't have any problems. You'll find a clean bed to sleep in. You can freshen up there in the morning and come here after you've had some tea. I had said—OK. What more does a salesman need! A shelter somewhere for the night. A room. Any woman. And in the end, sleep.

The woman wasn't bad. But she was completely broken. She said—If you have any spare cash, order a bottle of the local rum. After doing the rounds for an entire day in this industrial city, I had done business worth about 5000 rupees. 300 would be due to me as commission. A bottle of rum could be ordered. A large bottle of rum and chicken broth from the Punjabi hotel outside. The woman cheered up—Let the night fall, I'll make you happy. I'm not a cold woman. Once I heat up, then it's you who'll be in trouble . . .

There were other women, too, in that house. But Shamshad had said—Don't go to the others. Her name is Dipu. From Punjab. Go only to her. And I had come to Dipu.

I had said—Shamshad has sent me to you. I am a salesman from NuBuilt Company. I will go to Calcutta tomorrow morning. I want to stay the night. But I don't have a lot of money.

Shamshad who? The one from the Kashmiri hotel? Why didn't he come himself? He must have gone to the ugly madam next door. These days he goes only to her—Dipu answered with a long sigh and went away to give my 20 rupees to the landlord. Then she returned and said—If you have any spare cash, order a bottle of Indian rum. It will cost a total of 8 rupees. Alcohol and women are cheap here. See, no, when I do business, people happily pay 50 rupees for the whole night. I'm a hardworking woman. I know how to do things properly. Don't feel ashamed at all. Think of it like this: that in the dark, every woman is every man's wife. The dark erases shame. Colour, faith, caste, love, integrity, everything gets rubbed out in the dark. Only the woman below the waist remains.

Though it wasn't yet midnight, suddenly the police arrived. The main door was locked from the inside. The owner must have leant out of the window and confirmed that it was, indeed, the police. He came to Dipu's room and said—Dipu, the police've come. Run away with the customer! He went to the other rooms, told all the other women. You have to run away with the customer. Run where? Dipu said—Downstairs, underground. Let's go, we'll drink there, have a good time. Don't be scared, the police won't stay for long. Dipu was naked, I was also in an almost natural state. She wrapped a sheet around herself and said—Pick up the glass and come! Quickly!

There is a deep darkness in all directions, and we are sitting on the naked floor, awaiting light. When will the light come? Dipu unwraps the sheet from her body and lays it on the ground. She feels along the wall and keeps the bottle and the glass in a corner. Then asks—Who else is here? Chandravati, are you here? Nothing is visible in the dark. Not even one's limbs. And in this darkness, Dipu's voice shimmers like a white silver sword—Why don't you say something? The sounds from here can't be heard upstairs. And by now the owner must have paid off the police. Now why are you scared? Why not say something? Who else is here?

Who? Dipu the queen? You're here too? What kind of a customer do you have? Has he brought a bottle? Hey, give an ounce to me too. It's very cold here. Will you give me a little?—Some other woman breaks through the layers of darkness. I feel that spirit shadows are crawling about the room. A man steps on my thigh and jumps, scared—I thought it was an animal.

Of course, yes, it is an animal! What do you consider yourself? Human? Sir, only animals come here. Not human. Who are you?—Dipu laughs. Then the man lights up a match for a cigarette. He's wearing an overcoat. No hat. No shoes. Big, thick moustache. An angelic expression drips from his face. I ask—Who are you?'

I'm an engineer in a factory here. I'm alone, I had come here to pass the time. How could I have known that time will be spent in this basement—He lights a match again and starts looking at the other travellers in the room. It's a small room. The walls are naked. The floor is damp. A slender woman is lying in the corner, her head resting on her arms. An old man in a green lungi and a white shirt is standing silently in the middle of the room. Chandravati is lying in the lap of a young boy who looks like a student. That boy is caressing Chandravati's forehead. The match goes out. The engineer keeps circling the room. The heavy and stern sound of his shoes keeps echoing in the dark. The man standing in the middle of the room says—My money is gone. My woman is upstairs. I don't even have any alcohol. Not even a cigarette. Who knows for how long the police will create a ruckus upstairs?

The upstairs are really aflame. As if the roof will collapse. The police are perhaps searching the rooms. Maybe they are slapping the women who'd stayed upstairs. Maybe they're flogging the owner with a whip. Nothing can be known. Only that someone is running upstairs, that there are screams everywhere.

The student-like young boy screams in a delicate voice— Light a match. There's an insect in my trousers. Light a match! But no one lights a match. The engineer keeps strolling silently. Dipu moves towards me, gropes for the bottle and the glass. The glass breaks. The glass breaks because it's knocked over. I stumble. I feel along the floor and remove the big pieces of glass. There is a soft music in the sound of the glass pieces. Dipu opens the bottle, takes two gulps of rum, hands it to me the bottle and starts to cough. An old cough. Maybe it's asthma. Chandravati says—This is what happens when you drink alone . . .

I'll share, bitch. I'll give some to you, too! Don't abuse me like this—Dipu screams, then starts to cough. I try to straighten my frozen legs. Some rubber object is stuck between the toes of my right foot. I raise my leg and retrieve the object. People haven't forgotten to bring this rubber object even to the basement. Didn't forget even in the dark. I smile. After smiling, I try to pour the rum bottle down my throat. I don't know how much is left. Chandravati reels and falls into my lap, laughing. Dipu realizes it's Chandravati. She says—Look, Chandra, if you drink, you have to make this babu happy. This babu is from the same profession. We sell our skin, he sells sporting equipment made of leather . . .

My! You're totally naked—Chandravati starts giggling. Cheering up, I hand the bottle to her. Cheering up, she hands the bottle to Dipu. The bottle has been emptied and my head is spinning. That rubber thing is still in my fingers. My head is spinning. My nose is exploding from a bad odour. Bad odour from what? It seems many rats are lying dead around here. Chandravati has become an almost minute woman. I put my hand inside her blouse. It's as if nothing is there. Only a hanging piece of flesh. But the grip of her thighs is strong. Disgusted, I want to move away but I cannot. Both my legs are caged between her thighs. Large, bulging thighs! Heavy waist. Dipu says—Only military men come to this organ. This bitch breaks people. Now, Mister Salesman, How are you feeling?

I shrink. Chandravati uses force, I shrink. It seems like a dead rat is stuck between my thighs. Alcohol has turned me even colder. Just then the old man standing in the middle of the room starts to scream—Snake! A snake has bit me! Someone turn on the light . . . a snake has bit me . . . switch on the light . . . light . . .

But it does not get bright. The sound of the engineer's shoes stops. But no matchstick is lit. The boy accompanying

Chandravati blares—Light a match! Engineer-sahib, light a match. The snake will bite me . . . I killed a snake once! The snake will take revenge . . . save me . . . save me . . .

This has no effect on the engineer. He says—I have two cigarettes, and a total of two matchsticks. I will light a matchstick only when I feel like smoking a cigarette.

The end of the engineer's cigarette glows in the dark. His thick moustache glows. He is standing in a corner, leaning against the wall. And the boy is screaming. And Chandravati says—Let the old man die. He came here to enjoy himself instead of going to his grave. And Dipu says—It must be a rubber snake. Sultana from Room No. 8 had brought a rubber snake during the last police raid. We were all scared. Sultana's customer even fainted from fear.

It's not a rubber snake, it's real one! Blood is dripping from my foot. The poison is spreading. It's a venomous snake. It will bite everyone!—The old man keeps screaming, falls on the floor and writhes. Dipu laughs—Bastard! Writhing from fear . . . hey daddy . . . you're an old man . . . what difference will it make if you die? Hey Chandri what're you doing? Why don't you wrap it up quickly? Poor man has spent 8 rupees on alcohol . . . paid 20 in cash . . . the chicken meat was left upstairs . . . let the poor man enjoy! I'll also make a couple of moves . . . quickly Chandri . . . I'm heating up.

Now the engineer lights up the second cigarette. A piece of glass is buried in the old man's foot. Blood is really flowing. The old man is tossing his foot from side to side and screaming—I'm a coal stockist. If I die, people will enter the warehouse and take away all my coal . . . my son's turned out to be useless . . . he'll sell even the doors of the house and give all the money to whores . . . save me . . . let me go! Take me out of this basement!

By the light of the matchstick, the student-like boy has spotted the silent young girl against the wall. He is sliding towards her. The girl is frightened and quiet. The boy is perhaps trying to fill the void of Chandravati. The engineer extinguishes the matchstick and pulls at the cigarette with the full force of his chest. The empty alcohol bottle is buried between Dipu's thighs. Thighs as thick as wooden logs. Chandravati has trapped my neck between her hands and is shaking me— Hey mister, you also do something . . . what can I do alone? Use some force.

But I feel like I will faint now. This suffocation, this cold floor, the smoke from the engineer's cigarette, the stench of dead rats, the old man's screams, the bottle stuck between Dipu's thighs . . . I feel like I will faint now. Suddenly Dipu throws away the bottle and screams, You go, now you go Chandravati, you move! I will show this babu . . . go . . . fuck off . . . I will eat him alive.

And the rum bottle lands near the girl sitting against the wall. She screams in a shrill voice—I am dead. My head has exploded . . . I am dead . . .

The young boy leaps towards her like a hound. The engineer starts strolling again. The sound of his shoes is terrifying. Chandravati is gasping on the floor. Dipu has climbed on top of me. She is shaking me. I slowly drift off to sleep. Maybe I faint. Maybe I die. There is no recourse except to die.

ELEMENTARY KNOWLEDGE OF GEOGRAPHY

'Do you want to go see P. C. Sorcar's magic show? . . . splitting girls into half with a saw . . . enchanting spells . . . Sputnik show . . . are you going?' I asked Rama's mother. She was on the veranda, sitting on a palm-leaf mat, enjoying the hesitant sunlight of the first week of December. She smiled when she saw me, carefree as ever, in my blue half-pants and T-shirt and old muffler.

She turned towards me after moving a pillow beside her. Said, 'Rama has gone for his tuition. The boy is quite weak in maths. Why don't you help him?' Rama's full name is Ramavallabh Narayan Singh. However, he is the most beautiful and feminine boy in our school. We, meaning both of us, sit on the same double-desks of the 10th Standard's B section. The Hindi teacher, Mathura-babu, has named us: perfect pair! Once during recess, Mathura-babu called me and said, 'We are transferring Rama to the C section! Do you have any problem?'

Everyone knows that I wouldn't care even if he were transferred to the D section. I am quite a carefree kind of boy. I have longing neither for Rama nor for any beautiful and good thing. Apart from hockey and football, I don't long for any other game.

When Rama heard about his transfer, he started crying in front of all the other boys. He complained that if I were not with him, all the other boys would tease him, for something obscene.

I was staring at Rama's mother. In the almond light of the morning, her entire body was shimmering like a ray of sunlight. Her saree had slid upwards on the right side of her body. The health and amber of her thighs captivated me. My own mother usually keeps ill. It seems as if she will fall apart any moment at a mere touch. At night, she keeps coughing and rambling on about the world, family, god and my father. It looks as if she may not survive this horrific winter of 1944.

'Why are you so scruffy? . . . Doesn't Savitri wash your clothes? Why don't you oil your hair?' Rama's mother asked, seeing me standing in the same carefree manner. I decided for the seventeenth time that I should not stare at the naked ankles of this huge and heavy 32–35-year-old woman. Rama's mother's real name is Manmohini Devi! She is our neighbour. Rama's father was a police inspector. He died while fighting the dacoits of Rajauli-Neemantar. Manmohini Devi lives alone with her only child. She owns the house and has some ancestral property in the village. Father often says, 'Rama's mother has suffered a lot . . . if it were any other woman, she would have hung herself or ended up being a prostitute. Inspector-sahib drank two bottles of alcohol every day. Ate two kilos of mutton every day. Always laden with debt! . . . It was Rama's mother who somehow managed to run the household.'

But when the topic comes up, my mother Savitri Devi says things that are entirely different—things that I couldn't understand despite being in the 10th Standard. According to Savitri Devi, if it were her, she certainly would have saved her own husband! 'A chaste woman through her chastity could have . . . ! Our Manmohini is a modern woman, she chews tobacco despite being a widow, wears colourful sarees, and . . . ' My mother can never complete a sentence.

When I am standing in front of her, she doesn't talk about Rama's mother. She goes silent. She knows that Rama is my friend. She knows many things about me because she is my mother . . .

There are many homosexual boys in my class. These boys are usually the teachers' favourites. Rama, despite being feminine in his ways and form, did not like his teachers. Maybe because he was a city boy, his father was in the police . . . and he recognized the look in the eyes of his classmates and teachers.

He didn't even need a moment to understand what someone was thinking about him. As far as I remember, he knew how to take undue advantage of this understanding. He used to con rich boys into giving him money . . . but one couldn't call it conning because Rama was a coward and conning someone requires courage! Rama was scared of everyone except me. He used to trust me because I used to protect him from the other boys. He used to get into fights often because of this assurance. But not in my absence . . . Once in my absence, two boys from the 11th Standard bothered him a lot. Since then, he never left his house alone in the evening. He was, however, not a frail and weak boy. He was shapely and healthy. We were the best centre players in the school's football team. I have not seen another player who can run with the football as fast as Rama. And yet he couldn't make a goal even after managing to take the ball close to the goalpost . . . I have seen Rama looking hopeless several times, with the ball at his feet.

The football would have made it in with just a slight nudge but Rama's feet did not have even a little force . . . he would feel hopeless. On such occasions, I would snatch the football from his feet and make the goal. People would say, 'The perfect pair made five goals after half-time.' People used to say many things.

I felt neither good nor bad in Rama's company. At NCC camps and other such places, I had done some obscene things to Rama, sometimes in a huff or to impress the other boys. But I did not feel attracted either to him or to any other boy or girl. I preferred getting into fights, watching games and football. Often, I would slap Rama eight to ten times and stop going to his house.

Then his mother would come to our house to make up with me. My mother is scared of Manmohini Devi. She never says anything bad in front of her. It gives me pleasure to see my mother's double nature.

Suddenly Manmohini Devi stretched out her hands and snatched the muffler from my neck. Like the great warrior Karna had his protective armour, I have this muffler knitted by my aunt. This muffler made of red and yellow woollen coils protects me from many problems. In brawls and fights, in trapping someone's legs, in winding around someone's neck . . .

Once the muffler was snatched away, I felt like I was naked. Like blushing girls, I tried in vain to cover my neck with my hands . . . I had not taken a bath in four or five days. The muffler had been on me constantly, and that is why there were layers of dirt on my neck. The red rays of the sun started gliding on my suddenly exposed neck. I felt small insects crawling down my neck and hips. As if a thousand blisters had suddenly popped up. Writhing, I started rubbing my neck with my two claws, scraping the dirt, and sat on the mat with a sudden thump, near Rama's mother's feet! She was laughing at my state but her laugh disappeared as she saw me falling on the mat. 'Oh, what happened? . . . What happened?' she asked and sat up. She pulled me near her, placed my head and half of my upper body on her lap and began to caress me.

I closed my eyes. I told her, 'No, no . . . nothing has happened.' And I kept scratching my neck and my back. But I was laughing inside. My lips were curled up, my face had distorted from an imaginary sorrow and I was laughing inside at Manmohini Devi's concern. I had only pretended to fall on the mat with a thump. I've had to perform many such plays, big and small, since I was 8–10 years old.

When I accidentally break a glass, I stand in front of Mother and cry despite being the shrewdest and the most mischievous boy in my class. If I did not pretend to cry, Mother would utter some crass and utterly provincial maxim, and Father would call me to his room and give me a long and boring lecture for a full two hours about discipline, character building and ideal conduct. My father has memorized M. Smiles' book about character. After his lecture, he always repeats a story about an English boy who, obeying his father, stood in the corner of the ship and did not move even when the ship caught fire. 'Make that boy your model.'

'Good character is the greatest ornament of man. Every night, before sleeping, count all the good deeds you've done that day. Count also the mistakes.' After my every mistake, Father would repeat these saintly sentences worth framing on the wall. I was frightened of my mother's maxims and my father's lectures. So, in my defence, I had adopted these dramatic techniques . . . My mother Savitri's Devi's favourite saying was 'A faithful wife wastes away in the kitchen while the whore visits temples.' And she often used it for her friend and neighbour Manmohini Devi. My mother is an expert at coming up with sayings. These sayings help her win verbal wars against her neighbour. She also never misses a chance to use them on my father.

This is why I panicked when after snatching my muffler Rama's mother started sniffing it, because my muffler is drowned in sweat and scum and has a stench. I thought she would smell the odour and say 'ew' and throw it on my face. And ask me to leave.

Trembling with that fear, I pretended to fall down.

Manmohini Devi didn't throw the muffler at my face, instead she laid me on her lap and started caressing my neck. Then she said, 'Why Phool-babu, what happened? . . . did an insect bite you?' My eyes were closed and her shapeless, big breasts were swinging above my nose. I tried to look at them out of the corner of my eyes but I couldn't see anything. My eyes wouldn't open.

Phool-babu is my nickname. I can never remember the name composed of five words and eight ligatures that is recorded in the school register. I do remember Phool-babu. This flower boy, despite being 14 or 15, has not seen a woman so close . . . Rama's mother was leaning over my chest and face like a big rock. I was thinking about my name. Phool-babu, Ramavallabh, Priyadas-babu, the doctor's son Kaminidas, the boy from Bhushan-Bhavan Chaandmal—we were the best players on our school's football team and not all that interested in studying. I had not started smoking but I'd adopted every other vice thanks to Rama and Chaandmal. Chaandmal would steal money from his house. Then we would be faced with the problem of how to spend that money . . . Once our school's peon, who was almost our football team's manager, took us to Kamaalpur to drink palm wine. That day, Chaandmal had 20–25 rupees with him. In AD 1944, 25 rupees was a big sum.

After drinking palm wine, Sukhlal-peon asked for 10 rupees from Chaandmal and said, 'Sir, you people sit here. I'll be back in a minute . . . ' Kaminidas started smiling. Among us four friends, he was the eldest. He had a deep friendship with Sukhlal. He had visited Kamaalpur many times with Sukhlal. Kaminidaas understood where Sukhlal had gone with those 10 rupees . . . that's why he was laughing. And the three of us were quiet . . . This slum in the shade of a small cliff, surrounded by palm and date trees, Kamaalpur, was a colony of Pasis and Musahars. Under the shadow of the cliff—small huts made of hay and bamboo far from each other . . . dark and ugly women . . . naked children . . . ! A drove of pigs, roaming around. Inside our hut, four or five local-breed dogs. It's not yet dark but it will be soon.

Tipsy from the palm wine, Chaandmal says, 'Now I have 11 rupees left. Rama, you keep this money.' Rama looks at me. Chaandmal crams a 10-rupee note into Rama's hand. He puts the 1-rupee coin back in his own pocket and says, 'We'll have to keep 1 rupee for the rickshaw.' Rama extends the note to me. Kaaminidaas starts singing a Bengali song, 'O O bodhu sundari . . . kabe aasbe jamini, madhu jamini' (Oh beautiful bride, when will the night arrive, the honeyed night!) Chaandmal laid his head on Rama's thighs, wrapped his hands around his waist and fell fast asleep. That gesture angered me very much but my stomach was bloated due from too much palm wine, my limbs were growing limp . . . and at that moment I didn't at all feel like pulling that 40-kilo heavy boy away and dragging his corpse from Kamaalpur town to Patna Junction . . . Noticing my expression, Rama himself pushed Chaandmal away. The real event happened after Chaandmal blacked out.

After a while, Sukhlal-peon entered the hut with a cigarette between his lips. A woman of about 18–20 years of age followed him in. She sat down right in front of me and began trying to recognize each of our faces. Sukhlal said, 'Phool-babu, this hut belongs to her. Meaning, to her husband. These people are from the Pasi caste.'

Sukhlal started to smile faintly. She got up and poured herself a glass of palm wine. She drank two–three glasses of wine very quickly. Then she asked Sukhlal for a cigarette.

I panicked at the sudden appearance of this heroine on the stage. I gauged slightly why this woman had come. But I was doubtful. I placed the 10-rupee note back in my pocket and became alert. Sukhlal said, 'I have paid for the palm wine.

Everything cost about ten rupees. I have given a full seven rupees to this Pasi bird, meaning . . . this woman. One and half rupees each for all of you, one rupee for me! So, we agree?'

'Why won't we agree! These are studious boys from a government school . . . Why won't I agree?' The Pasi woman laughed and blushed as she drink the remaining palm wine in her glass. Then she started laying leaves in one corner of the hut.

Manmohini Devi caressed my arm and said, 'Come, come inside. Let me oil and bathe you. Come inside the house.'

. . . I stood up but then hesitated. Looking at Rama's mother swaying like a snake, insisting ('Come inside the house'), I am reminded of that Pasi woman laying the bed of palm leaves in the hut.

As soon as I remembered that, I felt like leaping onto the veranda, running away into the fields and screaming 'Help! Help me!' No, this whole thing about screaming for help was, to an extent, wrong . . . Though, it's true that, until the Pasi woman, I'd never had the experience of intercourse with a woman. Apart from my mother and father, I had seen my cousin and his wife indulge in these unsightly activities. The cousin's name was Bhavanand! And he was double my age. In my grandmother's house, I would sleep in the same room where his wife would come after everyone had gone to sleep . . . In the beginning, it seemed like they were fighting or beating each other. Then one day I realized they were doing the same thing that Hindi-teacher Mathura-babu had tried to do with Rama.

Bhavanand and his wife would start moaning like animals, jumping about, calling each other lewd names and almost wrestling. My grandmother, sleeping in the next room, would then start coughing loudly. Once it was raining. When a lightning bolt flashed and lit up the room, I saw by its light something that is perhaps best left unsaid. I'd closed my eyes out of fear. I felt as though my cousin's wife had climbed atop my cousin's chest and was trying to murder him. Afterwards, I had seen the image of the world mother Kali atop Shiva's chest . . . This first experience is etched in my mind like that.

As etched in my mind as the fear of Bhavanand's murder . . . The Pasi woman says, 'Sukhlal, go wait outside. What if my man returns?' Sukhlal, in a cheery mood, leaves the room. Kaaminidaas is staring greedily at the woman. He has tasted 'blood' before. He knows the taste . . . Chaandmal is sleeping, snoring. Rama now understands the whole game but he is scared, and he wants to move from his spot and come close to me.

'Who will go first?' The woman stands up. She stretches. Then takes off her saree, folds it, keeps it in a corner . . . It's not yet dark. By the last rays of the setting sun, this woman seems dark, like a silhouette, and very ugly.

Under the saree, she is wearing a red loincloth in the style of Hanuman. She repeats the question . . . Rama is sitting quietly beside me. I panic . . . Now what to do? Kaminidaas says, 'Phool-babu? . . . Phool-babu, should I go first?'

The Pasi woman had taken off the reins of her panties by then. 'Black mare, crimson reins,' I suddenly remembered the saying (heard from my mother). I had the intense desire to gag . . . to vomit all the palm wine inside my gut onto that woman's naked body. Then faint. But right then, the woman said, 'Hey, babu? Your name is Phool-babu, right? You come first.'

Rama gripped my arms, as if she had called him instead of me . . . Sukhlal-peon peaked inside, then signalled to us to finish the whole thing quickly.

My mother Savitri Devi . . . my cousin's wife . . . Rajvallabh . . . the Pasi woman . . . and now Manmohini Devi pressed my left arm and said, 'Sit on the bed. Don't hesitate! You are my son just like Rama is.' Then she pressed me close to her waist, sniffed my head and started patting my cheeks. I tried disentangling myself and took a step back, 'If you talk to Mother, surely she would let me go see the P. C. Sorcar magic show . . . Will you come? You, me and Rama?'

Manmohini Devi started laughing. Like mad women laugh . . . like my cousin's wife laughed atop Bhavanand-brother's chest . . . like the Pasi woman, taking me in her arms like a sack of potatoes, had said, 'My, my! What a lovely name, Phool-babu! Phool-babu! Let me take you on a plane ride.' . . . Manmohini Devi sat down on one corner of the bed, laughing. Then she said, 'I will take you wherever you want. Forget P. C. Sorcar . . . I will take you to England on a plane. There are big magicians there, they will turn you into a domineering, strong and tall young man of 25–26 in an instant, will you come with me? Come? C–O–M–E?'

I started screaming, 'I won't go. No, no, I won't go.' But no sound came out of my throat. I wanted to pretend to faint and fall on the ground. But it was as if someone had tied me to a steel pole. I couldn't move. I turned into ice, I froze . . . I shrank like the neck of a tortoise. I was in such a bad state that I couldn't even turn and look at Rama. Shame . . . marvel and terror. What else can be done now except to shut the eyes and let the water from the overflowing river pass over me!

I forgot to mention that I am even more cowardly than Rama. Rama at least had the courage to stand up and leave the hut. He didn't stay . . . I didn't even have that strength. I was scared.

This fear is in my blood. This blood also gives me the force to attack. When I feel scared, I do not run away. I try to attack at the right moment. The game of football is played on the same principle. Despite all possibilities of defeat, one must not run away. One should look for an opportunity. But even after accepting this principle, the truth is that I am a coward and I play football and do these mischievous acts to hide my fear.

I keep protecting Rama from the other boys because, internally, this blister keeps ripening—'I am a coward.' I am scared of everything in the world . . . I am happy when Rama is with me. I feel like I am not a coward because it is due to me that Rama goes to school and plays football.

However, Rama was not with me. I was alone and I felt enraged with Sukhlal-peon and Kaaminidaas pouring the rest of the palm wine into his mug. It's these two who have pushed me into the ghost-spectacle . . . now what is to be done? Oh god! Now what? I felt shards of glass sinking into my back.

In that one moment, I was filled with terror, anger, disgust, regret, pain and rage. I decided, 'Now I must save my life.' I decided, and then let my whole body loose, held my breath and started the pretence.

How does a man faint? He submerges slowly, 'sinks' and dies. How his weight, the blackness of his body, the poison of his eye increases! I knew all this.

When no other pretence works, I pretend to die. The same pretence as Shiva, lying under the empress Kali . . . My pupils stilled, my breath stopped, my hands, legs, knees . . . the entire grammar of my body went cold, like a dead black snake. My body's grammar . . . my gender, form, liaison, compound, everything.

Manmohini Devi tried to revive me and warm my body. She said, 'Don't worry, Phoolbabu . . . let me massage you . . . let me massage you with the fragrant Mahabhringraj oil.'

But the snake was dead . . . I picked up the muffler lying on the bed and wrapped it around my neck.

A CHAMPA BUD: A VENOMOUS SNAKE

Dashrath Jha has a small family but a big courtyard. Earlier, all the brothers lived together. Now, Dashrath Jha has been left alone with his wife and children in this huge, derelict courtyard filled with a jungle of marijuana and moonflower. Dashrath's means of livelihood is—a buffalo. This one buffalo provides about 8 to 10 litres of milk every two days. Apart from the buffalo, he has one and a half bighas of land—and nothing else. His wife—she's from Ramganj—keeps busy with the household, one child is in school, another child is in buffalo, meaning, grazing the buffalo, and in the last stage of her twelfth year, graceful, tender, courteous, obedient, cheerful—their only daughter.

The daughter's name is Champa.

When the 62-year-old Shashi-babu came and stood in the middle of Dashrath Jha's courtyard, his closest neighbour and distant relative, Champa was arranging the dung cakes. The Ramganjwali was near the well . . . As soon as she saw Shashi-babu, she picked up her bucket of water and went into the kitchen. According to village relations, Shashi-babu was like a father-in-law to her.

Dashrath Jha, laughing, boomed in a welcoming voice, 'Why do you feel shy? Shashi-babu is like family . . . Champa, tell your mother to arrange for a pot of water. By water, I mean hot water.'

'Why hot water, Father?' Champa asked softly. Equally softly, Champa's mother replied from the kitchen, 'Hot water means tea. Champa, go and get tea and sugar from the shop. I'll put the water on the boil.'

There is nothing that disturbs Champa more than going to the shop. Each time she returns from the market, Champa swears that she would rather die than come again. If something has to be borrowed, whether it's two ounces of supari or two pounds of mustard oil—it's always Champa who is sent to the shop. Champa objects: 'I won't go. One and half rupees is due to the grocer. He won't lend me anything.'

But Mother or Dashrath say, 'If you won't go, who will? Champa, tell the grocer that I won't swallow his 1 rupee. Potatoes will be plucked tomorrow. We will sell them and give him his rupee.' Champa knows that Father has not sown even a hundred yards of potatoes. Champa knows that Father lies sometimes, about small things, he lies, utter lies.

However, the most prestigious person of Dakshinbaria area has come to the courtyard, that too for the first time— Father must have some important business with Shashi-babu, Champa guesses. She has the womanly capacity to know this. And so Champa, without even answering her mother—went to the grocer's—as beautiful as a statue of a goddess, a young, intelligent and courteous girl, Champa! Dashrath goes into the eastern room with Shashi-babu. Champa, Champa's mother and Dashrath live in this house.

An old calendar is hanging on the wall. An illustration on the calendar. Shashi-babu, as if waiting to hear about some important matter from Dashrath, stares at the picture for a long time. Draupadi is helpless, half-clothed . . . Dasaratha mad with rage . . . Duryodhana blinded by pride . . . the five Pandavas with their heads hanging in shame and remorse . . . and Krishna draping Draupadi with swathes of saree from above . . .

Radha's almighty lover Krishna is smiling pleasantly in that calendar illustration.

Shashi-babu also smiled but internally, and said nothing. However, it was not difficult for Dasaratha to understand that Shashi-babu was pleased to be in this house, sitting on this old bed in this room. Dasaratha Jha needs this pleasure. Shashi-babu, till a few years ago, had been the head clerk in Purnea District Court. Now he lives permanently in the village. Shashi-babu's family is large. Two widowed sisters, four sons from three wives and families, large and small, of those four sons. Nothing has been divided up until now. As long as Shashi-babu is alive, division is impossible.

Despite being married three times, Shashi-babu is at present wifeless. The third wife passed away five years ago. Shashi-babu is now old, yet he manages all the household expenses. He keeps the keys to his trunk tied to his sacred thread.

'If you won't help us, who will?' Dasaratha started with this love-laden sentence. Shashi-babu had taken out his tobacco box from his pocket and was chewing paan and tobacco. After closing the box and placing it back in his pocket, he said, 'I will do whatever I can, of course I will, but tell me clearly . . . how much money do you need . . . how much at least?'

Dasaratha Jha calculates in his mind. Expenses for Champa's wedding, how much should be asked from Shashi-babu? 700? 1,000? Dasaratha Jha would need at least 2,000 to get his daughter married into an 'ordinary' family. After calculating, Dasaratha said, 'First have some tea, we'll talk money later. And what can I say, my wife will talk to you her-self. What is hidden from you . . . what shame from you . . . you are our own people.'

Dasaratha Jha has a perfectly appropriate boy in mind for Champa. He is friends with the boy's father. Bharathpur vil-lage, 10 kilometres north of Saharsa. The boy is studying BA at Saharsa College. Ramganjwali has calculated everything. At least 1,500 could be earned from selling 150 yards of land. Three asharfis of gold jewellery are already at home. If Shashi-babu can arrange even 500 . . .

After keeping the sachets of tea and sugar next to her mother, Champa stood on the veranda. It will not be too long before it is evening. In the afternoon, it had rained—torrential rains, mud in the courtyard . . . mud on the streets . . . Champa had slipped and fallen while going to the shop. Mother said, 'Change your saree and tie your hair . . . hurry up. Shashi-babu is not going to be here for long. Tie your hair . . . there's a saree on the clotheslines . . . wear that . . . hurry up. Go and give tea and paan to Shashi-babu.'

Champa went to the well. She filled the bucket with water. She washed herself for a long time. Removed the turmeric stain from her elbow. Dirt near the temples . . . dirt near her eyebrows . . . but there is no dirt on Champa's body, only an illusion of dirt exists in her mind. A little while ago, when she fell near the shop . . . Abhimanyu Chaudhary's nephew Parixit had laughed so hard . . . she felt tainted with shame, with shame, anger, humiliation. She suspected that Parixit had even used a bad word. Even if Parixit had merely laughed and not said anything. Champa, at this young age, feels distressed and worried at the mere suspicion of dirt, bad words and humiliation.

After washing herself, she came to the veranda near the kitchen to search for the red saree and red blouse. If Mother says so, then she must powder herself, arrange her hair, wear a red saree and hand a cup of tea to Shashi-babu. Whatever Mother says must be done. And that's what Champa does. Even if she doesn't want to . . . like going to the shop . . . like going to Lalitesh's courtyard . . . many things that Champa does not feel like doing. Champa doesn't want to enter that room in which Shashi-babu is sitting on the bed and Champa's father, Dasaratha Jha, is sitting on a stool below, in a gesture of flattery and persuasion. Champa is not ashamed . . . but she feels disgust, sorrow about why her father is like this . . . so poor and minuscule . . . Why is Father not sitting on the bed? . . . Due to what selfish reason is tea being made for Shashi-babu? . . . Why is Mother so unsettled?

'You wait, I will be back in two minutes,' said Dasaratha Jha and came out on the veranda, picked up a pot and left the courtyard. Shashi-babu is looking at the disrobing of Draupadi on the calendar and wondering if money should be lent to Dasaratha Jha or not. It is most likely that the money will be lost. However, if money is not lent, then how will Champa get married? . . . And where did Dasaratha go? He said his wife would talk to me herself? Why would she talk to me?

In front was the wife with a plate of halva in one hand, a glass of water in the other . . . and behind her, hidden, in a red saree and red blouse, a demure and hesitant Champa . . .

The wife has not covered her head. There is, undoubtedly, beauty in her big eyes but no womanly shame. Shame is the inner flame of the female eye . . . It is as if the wife's eyes are created out of stone, beautiful, but without any allure. Taking the cup of tea from Champa's hand, Shashi-babu felt her tremble . . . as if every part of her body was shaking. Her forehead damp with sweat . . . her eyes shimmering with tears. Shashi-babu felt that if Champa stood here for one more moment, she would fall down in a faint.

Champa didn't wait for any new orders from Mother. After handing the cup of tea to Shashi-babu, she silently walked out of the room, giving Mother a sharp look of disregard, then paused in the courtyard for a moment, then went out to her friend Annapurna's. Whenever Champa feels drowned in sorrow, she goes to Annapurna's house and falls asleep.

'Dasaratha didn't say anything about money . . . how much is needed and what else, whatever is needed, only you can tell me,' said Shashi-babu, surprised and relieved by Champa's swift exit. Then 'Where is Dasaratha?' he asked.

'He has gone towards the bathaan, where we tie the buffaloes,' the wife said, 'He'll be back any moment . . . but his presence and absence is irrelevant. He hesitates to say anything to you. He will not. But I will. Champa is my daughter, I am Champa's mother. Only the mother has any right on the daughter—not the father. A mother sacrifices her life for her daughter. I do, too. This is why I will talk to you.'

Shashi-babu feels apprehensive at the wife's cogent, courageous and clear speech. What does Dasaratha's wife want to say? Shashi-babu straightens himself up and places a pillow under his back. Why did Dasaratha leave? Why did Champa run away? Why is the wife talking so intimately? What is she building a preface to? Shashi-babu is not from the village, he has spent all his life in the city. He is an urban man, Shashi-babu. After leaving his job, he has shifted permanently to the village. But he is not acquainted with rural rituals, rural politics, rural people's customs, language, behaviour. This is why Shashi-babu doesn't have the appropriate capacity to understand the nuances of the wife's preface.

Shashi-babu, holding a paan, opens the tobacco box. He is waiting to hear the actual point. The wife goes back to the courtyard. Where has Champa gone? Is any woman from the neighbourhood around? The wife returns to the room.

'Now I am getting late . . . Where is Dasaratha?'

The wife smiles. Says, 'At least 2,000 to 2,250 will be needed for Champa's wedding, we only have 1 bigha and 10 kathas of land. And one buffalo. If we sell 10 kathas, we'll get 500.'

Shashi-babu interrupted, 'Why would you sell the buffalo? Why would you sell the farm? And if you do sell, how would you live?'

The wife possibly wanted to hear this exact question. So, as soon as he asked it, she laughed. Laughed in the contented manner of a heroine from a play with a happy ending, then said, 'You are right. If I sell all of this for my daughter's wedding, then I won't manage to live. It's not wise to take away bread from one's own mouth, I know this much. This is why we, meaning my lord, my daughter and I seek your refuge . . . Only you, only you can save us.'

'Only you can save us . . . ' As soon as he heard these words from the wife's mouth, Shashi-babu grew disenchanted. He felt enraged at having wasted his time here. Since the last few days, Dasaratha Jha has repeated this sentence a thousand times, that only Shashi-babu can save him and his family.

However, it was not for saving but for his own self-interest that Shashi-babu had come at this strange hour, all alone, to Dasaratha Jha. Shashi-babu always plans everything. How to play the chess of life, how to turn a living person into a wooden pawn or knight or bishop. He knows the secret to this.

Shashi-babu's house is quite small. The family is large. And Dasaratha Jha's courtyard is adjacent to Shashi-babu's western wall. If Dasaratha Jha sells 400 square feet of the northern part of his land, he won't mind paying 1,000–1,200 as payment for Champa's wedding. Shashi-babu hasn't come to Dasaratha Jha's courtyard to save anyone but to buy 400 square feet of land. And so, the wife's words didn't please him.

35

He grew irritated that she was wasting so much time on the preface and not getting to the main story . . . People would pointlessly wonder why Shashi-babu was sitting alone in a room in his neighbour's courtyard.

After a long time, after calming herself, taking a serious stance, somewhat astonished, the wife said, 'I will not sell the farm. I will not sell the house. I cannot sell the buffalo. I don't just have Champa—I have other children, too. Their mouths can't be muzzled.'

Shashi-babu asked, 'If you won't sell the house, what will you do? How much money will you take from me?'

The wife answered, 'Not a lot, we will take 1,500 rupees in cash. And whatever jewellery, clothes, sarees you want to give to Champa, that's your will. Champa will always be happy with rich, wise and cultured people like you. She will always be happy . . . '

'Only you can save us'—Shashi-babu now understood its real meaning. This is why such a long preface was being composed. Shashi-babu himself should marry Champa—that is the real objective of Dasaratha Jha and his wife. The wife herself has planned this. If the 60-year-old handsome, healthy, courageous old man Shashi-babu marries the 13-year-old vain, shy, virgin, young champa bud, then Dasaratha Jha and his wife will possess the lawful right, the sole right to Shashi-babu's entire business, entire wealth, and, as queen consort, Champa will rule old Shashi-babu's world like a queen, my Champa, my champa bud.

Champa had handed him the tea. Shashi-babu certainly took a liking to her, my daughter, my lovely young daughter. Such big eyes, such a pure simple nature. No one else's daughter in the whole village has such a sharp mind and intelligence.

Of course, joking on the veranda with his group of friends, Shashi-babu had once said that he felt like getting married again. But that had been a joke, not the truth. At this strange age of 62, Shashi-babu doesn't have any wish to get married. He is a freeheart, now he won't entangle himself in anything.

And so, he got off the bed, stood on the ground and said in a harsh tone, 'I heard what you said. Tell Dasaratha Jha that I am not so stupid. Not a lot, Champa is only 22 years younger than my daughter Kalyani. And four years younger than my daughter's daughter, Munni. How much older am I than Champa? How much younger than me is your husband? . . . How did such a thought enter your mind?'

The wife gave Shashi-babu a poisonous look of immense indifference. Shashi-babu felt terrified. As if it was not a woman standing in front of him but a venomous snake, in a vicious stance . . . a frightening venomous snake . . .

The wife didn't answer Shashi-babu. Not a sentence, not a word. A venomous snake's answer is in its venom, its sac of venom!

But what is this law of the universe that, in this social situation, it is not Shashi-babu who is the venomous snake— the venomous snake is Champa's mother!

AN ANGRY MAN

The June of 1965 had not yet passed. It had been many years since we'd had such beautiful summer afternoons. Sweat forms on the body and evaporates off the hot pan. The body doesn't burn, the clothes are hot pans. Yet, at exactly six in the evening, they came to the tea cabin. This restaurant is built on the port, on the roof of the station building. Built in the likeness of a ship, this restaurant keeps floating on the blue surface of the Ganges.

Kamlesh arrived first. Then Mahtab Ali. Ramnath arrived last, whereas he had to arrive early to occupy the corner seat from where one has the best view of the ship's passengers. The ladders of the ship can be seen. Women descend in a slow pace from the top deck, walking carefully, avoiding the crowds, holding a thermos, or a bag, or a child.

As soon as the ship docked, the blue-uniformed, red-turbaned porters jumped on it at a speed faster than ancient pirates pouncing on their prey ships. Every porter wants a First Class passenger. Third Class passengers now usually carry their own luggage. For an instant, the women descending from the ship are lost in a crowd of blue uniforms.

This one instant, for Kamlesh, is an instant of anger towards the porters and the women.

Most of his evenings are spent in this tea cabin. He comes straight here from his newspaper office, the newspaper is a weekly, and the regional minister of the Industry and PWD Department has invested money in it. After looking at the page proof, Kamlesh takes a rickshaw, sits at the corner table of this restaurant and waits for the 6 p.m. steamer to arrive. There is no reason for his wait. No stranger or friend is arriving by the 6 p.m. steamer.

Students from Darbhanga district would arrive during their holidays, and Congress leaders as well as deputies would arrive when the State Legislative Council reopened. In the winters, the courtesans of Muzaffarnagar would come to Patna to spend their weekends. During the wedding season, brides from northern Bihar arrive, and the whole port drowns in sweating vermilion faces and red-yellow sarees. In the eyes of the brides feigning shyness: kohl, and vulgar curiosity. Kamlesh, drinking tea, keeps watching the return of the steamer ship. He will keep watching it every evening.

This is why he has come straight here, because he likes coming here more than anything else. For the past few months, Kamlesh hasn't liked being at home, drinking tea made by Saanvli and listening to her million complaints. He wants to tell every friend and visitor who comes home that Saanvli is not a wife, but a mere maid. He can't say it due to his nature. After many years of constant hard work, he has mastered reticence, keeping silent about almost everything.

Mahtab Ali straightened his round cap, pulled up a chair and said—This is totally wrong! I have come here after fighting with my boss, yet Mr Ramnath is nowhere to be found! He gets off at three, so where is he?

—He will come—Kamlesh smiled and ordered tea for Mahtab Ali. He refused. There is no point in having tea in this weather. When everything here is done, then beer shall be had at Central. Mahtab Ali is a father of three beautiful children studying at St Xavier's. He is a high official in Life Insurance Corporation. Just five years ago, he started out as an ordinary agent. This year, he will buy his own car. At the moment, he is building a small one-storey house on a plot in Rajendra Nagar. He is not old, but a rather big moon has emerged on the middle of his head. Mahtab Ali wears a round cap and goes to the cinema or shopping every Saturday with his wife and sisters-in-law. Kamlesh, despite a long friendship of 10 years, has never been to Mahtab Ali's house. Mahtab Ali had invited him for the wedding of his wife's eldest sister, Salma. Salma was known by the entire university for her beauty and style. Many people had crashed her wedding just to catch a glimpse of her draped in bridal clothes. Kamlesh didn't go. He had already started coming to the port every evening.

—Have you seen her husband? What kind of a man is he?—Mahtab Ali asked with a smile, then suddenly turned serious. Kamlesh wasn't thinking about her husband, he was thinking about his maid. It has not even been six months yet, and Saanvli has already become the mistress of the house. Mistress and head of the household. Yesterday, she almost slapped Gauri. Gauri, Kamlesh's younger sister, is here to study for her Inter. She was wearing frocks till just the other day. Must be about 14–15. After being admonished by Samresh, Saanvli Devi went into the kitchen and started crying.

—Have you seen her husband?—Mahtab Ali asked again.

Kamlesh responded—I had been to her wedding. I wouldn't have, but Ramnath started crying. He would not go himself but wanted to send a gift through me.

Kamlesh had reached late at Sarla's wedding. All the rituals had been completed. Guests were being introduced to the bride and groom, Sarla spotted him standing in a corner of the tent, silently smoking a cigarette. She dragged her husband to him. Laughing, blushing, she said, This is Kamlesh! He's a big journalist in the city. Why Kamlesh-ji, won't you publish at least one picture in your newspaper? And here, this is Mr Shibbanlal-ji. Class One Income Tax officer. He's started to boss me around already.

Kamlesh smiled at this sweet quip. He slowly held out the present, a packet wrapped in silken georgette. He had brought a tie clip in the latest style for Shibbanlal Kapoor. The saree had been sent by Ramnath, Sarla understood without being told. But she didn't feel morose. She brushed off the entire thing. Said, Do you know Kamlesh-babu, not even a bird from the radio station has come to my wedding! Everyone is boycotting! Tell me, what is the great crime in getting married!—Then she put her hand on Mr Kapoor's shoulder. She was neither taller nor shorter than him.

—Arrey! Ramnath is still not here?—Mahtab Ali said, staring at the door. Kamlesh kept drinking his tea silently, kept his head low. Ramnath is a producer of plays in the Patna

Radio station. He might be late. The Assistant Station Director takes a personal interest in the plays.

Kamlesh smiled. Why is Mahtab Ali being so impatient? Why does he want Ramnath to come here soon, his hair dishevelled, his years-old sorrow glued to his freshly shaven face, repeating his and Sarla Mathur's tale? For the past seven months, Ramnath has not talked about anything else. Every one of his friends knows every little detail. He has recounted even the smallest incident many times. Sarla doesn't sweeten her tea. She alone bears the expenses of the entire family. Her father, he spends the whole day playing rummy with the colony's elderly. Her five siblings, at various stages of school and college. We went to Delhi together for the interview. We took pictures at India Gate and Mughal Gardens. It was decided that we would marry as soon as Sarla's job was confirmed, my sisters had even started to call her 'Sister-in-law'. We spent entire nights counting the waves of the Ganges from the Krishna Ghat. Sarla laughed, blossoming and swaying like a yellow frangipani. She would say—I will have eleven children, Ram! Six boys and five girls. All six boys will be IAS officers. I will turn into a museum surrounded by five sons-in-law and six daughters-in-law!

Uff, Sarla said so many things! Ramnath would fall silent while recounting the tales. His eyes would turn to stare at the roof. Tainted lines of sleep on his face. He would slouch with his arms spread across the table and declare with the pride of lovers from the Mughal period, But the whole mistake is mine! Meaning, not anyone else's! It was my stupidity that changed the whole thing! . . . I have lost the game, friends, I am lost.

Kamlesh will smile. He will smile at the things said by the hero of this modern love story. He won't say anything, only smile. The others will dig around for everything, ask about every single thing, for example, what remark did the ASD make when he saw Sarla Mathur—announcer of English programs—and Mr Ramnath Rastogi—producer of Hindi plays—cling to each other's bodies in the dark corridor like sculptures of stone? Ramnath turns serious at this question. That magnificent woman sculpted from white marble, Sarla Mathur! The ASD had said—Well, where did the Khajuraho statue come from? Who brought this statue?—Listening to his boss' sarcasm, Ramnath had turned even more to stone. But Sarla carefully disentangled herself. Straightening her saree, she went towards the Assistant Station Director. Said with a smile—Khajuraho statues are the most excellent specimens of our country's art, sir.

Sarla was a fearless, witty and kind girl. Each staff member of the radio station loved her and, somewhere in their minds, also respected her. When she was asked to do anything, if she could, she would do it. Knit a sweater for you. Admit Mr Sharma's wife to the hospital. Organize a gala evening of refreshments, folk music and poetry at Mrs Rambahadur's. Everyone was happy with her. Her open laugh, her extremely sweet conversations . . . Ramnath Rastogi first had dinner with Sarla Mathur at the Broadway hotel. The next day, the news created an uproar at the radio station. Ramnath had kept sitting in his chair, his head held high with pride. Obviously, everyone was jealous of his luck. Sarla never paid any attention to envy of others. Every evening, after finishing her duty, she started going home with Ramnath in a rickshaw.

It was during those days that Kamlesh had written a song. Ramnath liked it so much that he attached his own name to it and used it in a play. Sarla Mathur had played the lead role in that play. She had sung that song, too:

The river of silence drowned in the whirlpool,
Like an entire epoch drowned in the whirlpool.

It was still half an hour till the steamer's arrival. People at the surrounding tables were drinking tea and talking about the weather and inflation. At one table, two students had been discussing for the past 15 minutes whether Pritibala was Madhubala's sister or not, and in which unfinished films of Madhubala had Pritibala worked as her 'dummy'. When Mahtab Ali felt totally fed up with all this noise (he was anyway getting angry with Kamlesh's silence and Ramnath's absence), he got up and went to the students' table. He said firmly—Do you know me? No?—then he sat down on the empty chair.

Both the students, who had agreed on an answer among themselves and begun to verbally describe in detail the physical characteristics of Madhubala and Pritibala, trembled at this firm question and then, shaking their heads, answered simultaneously—No.

—My name is Abdul Rehman. Pritibala, whose real name is Zeb Rehman, is my wife. She is not related to Madhubala. Now do you understand?—Mahtab Ali said in a peaceful, melodic voice and then stood up. Returned to his table. Kamlesh understood his mischief but did not even smile. With his head turned away, he kept looking at the blue waters of the Ganges. The month of June will end in a couple of days but it has still not rained. Not even a drop of water. Ma has written from the village that if it doesn't rain in the next four days, the villagers will go mad.

Kamlesh's mother teaches in her village school. She is also a member of the Congress Party. She doesn't want to come and live in Patna. When Kamlesh's wife was in hospital, she came for a week but then returned because there was an election in the village for the village head. When Kamlesh's wife fell ill, she just died, she never came back from the hospital. He kept publishing his minister-master's newspaper. Kept visiting his friends. He was saddened by Satya's death but Kamlesh bears silently that which he cannot escape. The song about the river of silence was written during those days, he had forgotten it, he only remembered four lines:

Spiderwebs on white walls
Fragments of butterfly wings on doors
Someone left silently after affixing
Kohled fingerprints on glasses

Those lines forced him to spend more and more time at home. Gauri has arrived just recently. Samresh, his younger brother, has been living with him for quite some time. He is in MA Final Year. He tops the class. After his wife's death, the two brothers started eating out at hotels. Even his home turned into a hotel. Then, when his friend was transferred to Travancore, he brought his maid to Kamlesh's home. She will cook, do laundry, stay in some corner somewhere. Mahtab Ali had advised against it. He'd said—In a bachelor's house, the maid quickly turns into the mistress! Instead of hiring a young maid, go to your village and get married. How long will you eat food cooked by a maid? You're not even a father yet.

45

This dark-faced, white-eyed woman was quite sharp and radiant. She did everything on her own. She kept account of each and every paisa, and when she went to buy ration and vegetables, she would treat herself to a magahi paan worth 2 annas yet never steal a single anna, nor ask for commission from the milk boy. She refused to lend 5–10 rupees to the neighbourhood women, even with interest. But if Gauri visits a friend's house and comes home late, Saanvli takes the vicious stance of a snake and says to her, If you return late, sister, I'll get you beaten up by your elder brother! Such big girls do not stay out late! If Gauri gets angry, so be it. Saanvli would lecture her in pure Hindi for 15 minutes.

Once, a Montessori drawing teacher, Daya Ben came to Kamlesh's house with him. She was a simple woman, with a peaceful disposition. She had come all the way to Patna from Gujarat for a job. Kamlesh had been to Daya Ben's schools for some children's events. He had even published pictures of those events in his newspaper. But Saanvli, to avoid making tea for this simple Daya Ben, started pretending there was no sugar in the house. Saanvli was very upset at this woman's visit. After Daya Ben left, Kamlesh's anger exploded on Saanvli. She started howling. She cried for a long time—I will not let the Gujaratan come to my house! I know she wants to marry you! I know . . . I will not let you get married to that old girl . . . !

Thankfully, Samresh wasn't home then. If he were, he would have dragged that black rock made of black stone out of the house. He would have thrown her out on the footpath. Samresh had done so many times. But each time, like a pet cat, Saanvli had returned at dinnertime to cook.

The two boys praising Pritibala and Madhubala had paid
their bill and left. The crowds waiting for the steamer had
started to swell. Mahtab Ali was humming a Ghalib couplet.
He was searching for the familiar face of Ramnath Rastogi
amid the crowd of incoming visitors. In his round cap and
with a sparse black beard on the lower part of his cheeks, he
looks more like an aristocrat from Lucknow and less like a
Life Insurance Corporation officer.

Kamlesh said, Ramnath should come any moment now.
It's almost time for the steamer to arrive . . .

Kamlesh hadn't even finished his sentence when Mahtab
Ali screamed—Finally, here is Mr Lover the Great!

Ramnath was running towards the table. Gasping, wiping
his face with a handkerchief, he sat on the empty chair facing
Kamlesh. I am really sorry! My friends, I am sorry that I am
late! It so happened, Kamlesh, that the Station Director had
locked me inside my room. How I have escaped, only I know!

Mahtab Ali thought Ramnath was making excuses, so he
asked, Why did he lock you? Your SD is a decent man. He
reads the namaaz four times. Eats vegetarian food. Why did
he have to take the path of violence?

—Listen, waiter, bring Coca-Cola for three. Don't be late!
And see, a packet of Gold Flake too—Ramnath said, then put
the handkerchief back in his pocket and faced Mahtab Ali—
Oh well, the news has spread in the radio station that Sarla
Mathur, who is now Sarla Kapoor, is returning for the first
time from her marital home and I am going to meet her at the
steamer port. Mrs Rambahadur said to the ASD, and the ASD
told the SD: it's possible that Ramnath might throw acid on

Sarla. Gangadhar Singh from the music department went so far as to say that I was carrying my uncle's revolver and going to the steamer port. That's why SD locked me in my room. Somehow, I have escaped . . .

—Why are you talking like a child, Ramnath!—Kamlesh said, wrinkling his nose. Ramnath fell silent.

When Kamlesh wrinkles his nose, his friends fall silent. If someone gave a topsy-turvy answer, Kamlesh would stand up and leave without another word. With his friends, with his colleagues, Kamlesh has always done this. Once when the Chief Editor said something stern to him, he left that 10-year-old permanent job and came away to this new newspaper. He's never learnt to compromise. If he could have learnt to bend a little, tolerate, Kamlesh wouldn't have been here, he would have been at some high post at some high office.

—You're not a little three-year-old boy, Ramnath, that you can be locked inside a room! I have been counting the waves for the past hour! Mahtab Ali is so bored that he is playing practical jokes on college boys. But Mr Ramnath Rastogi, MA, is nowhere to be found!—Kamlesh uttered this long monologue in a slow and strung-like-a-bow voice and started lighting a Charminar cigarette.

Mahtab Ali started smiling, He is being thrashed nicely, he thought.

Ramnath wanted to give a somewhat harsh answer but his mouth didn't open. He couldn't say, Kamlesh, Sometimes your wild nanny locks you inside a room too . . .

In fact, Kamlesh was angry with Saanvli and not with Ramnath. He had been thinking about his younger sister Gauri and his maid Saanvli and not about Sarla Mathur who is now Sarla Kapoor. Till late at night, lying on his bed, he reads newspapers, Hindi and English, from everywhere. Every day, he brings back 10 to 20 daily, weekly, monthly magazines and journals from his office. Gauri is reading some book, the lights were still on in the small room next door. She will keep reading for a long time. Samresh has made his bed in the courtyard and fallen asleep after switching off the light. Now even if the house is on fire, he won't wake up.

But until Kamlesh falls asleep, Saanvli will keep sitting on the floor, in the corner of his room, and ask strange questions. She babbles whatever comes to mind—Last evening, some religious man was lecturing on the intersection that in Russia there is no difference between a master and a servant. Poor or rich, everyone is equal there! Do you know, Kamlesh-babu, the Bengali woman next door has bought a radio worth 700 rupees. You should also buy a radio. Gauri likes listening to music so much! I want to . . . learn a little bit of accounting, a little Hindi from her. You bring me a ledger, I will record household expenses. Otherwise it's impossible to know how much money is being spent, how much is saved—When Kamlesh will fall asleep while silently reading the newspapers, Saanvli will switch off the lights. She will go outside.

Saanvli sleeps on the veranda in the cold, in the rains, in every season. Kamlesh has asked her many times to sleep in Gauri's room but she sleeps only on the veranda.

—Gauri sleeps with her room locked. If you need water or tea at night, who will bring it?—Saanvli asks, feigning great innocence. She arranges the woven mat on the veranda for herself. If he has to write at night, then Kamlesh needs tea at least once. He doesn't want to wake this dark woman sleeping on the veranda. But she wakes up herself. She tiptoes into the room, like a cat. If Kamlesh is sleeping, she switches off the light and tiptoes out. But if he is awake, writing, she says— Why, babuji, should I make a cup of tea?

This woman stays awake till three in the morning for me . . . this plump, young, animal-like woman. This thought angers Kamlesh. Satya, his wife never did so. Reading detective novels and falling asleep while reading, that had been her habit. She slept in another room, where Gauri sleeps now. She was an average comfort-loving Bihari woman. She made the servant from the village do all the household chores. Every second or third month, the servant would steal something and run away.

That is why Kamlesh was angry. Saanvli wasn't in front of him, that is why he took out his anger on Ramnath. Mahtab Ali said—Kamlesh-bhai is right, Ramnath-ji, you are not a three-year-old child! If you had gotten married timely, you would have had half a dozen children like me!

Ramnath became sullen. Mucky smoke from the ship was visible on the chest of the river. A small girl sitting at the next table started screaming,—The ship is coming . . . Mummy, look, the ship is coming!

After drinking Coca-Cola, the three friends came out onto the balcony. They stood against the railing. The steamer is now visible, like a white paper boat. Sometimes it hides in the smoke, sometimes in the blue water. Kamlesh's mind is also a white paper boat. This boat doesn't drown in the waves, it manages to float up each time.

Ramnath doesn't come upstairs. His eyes are fixed on the small steamer. As if suddenly he is different and beyond his two wise friends. He has accomplished only one thing in exchange for his entire peace of mind—love.

—After the Duke of Windsor, there is no other example of such great love in the twentieth century!—Ms Solanki would say to the duty officer while drinking coffee in the duty room of the radio station. With his head lowered like Hamlet's ghost, his shoulders slouched, Ramnath would stroll onto the veranda alone. He would unlisten to Ms Solanki.

The duty officer, slapping Ms Solanki's arm, said—Why so! Bombay's Ahuja affair was also like this, based upon which the film *Such Are the Ways of Love* was made. If our hero wants, he can fire at Shibbanlal Kapoor . . . !

Ramnath had overheard this. All the detective stories he'd read recently started floating in his mind—How the English robber Arsène Lupin murders the millionaire widow Mrs Hilda Comfort by mixing snake venom in her cup of hot coffee; the injection the Count of Monte Cristo gave his enemy Lord Fairfield that turned him mad; the magic Miss My Lady used; under the effect of which medicine did Dr Jekyl turned into Mr Hyde . . . But Ramnath didn't have the ability to do any of these things. He would have committed suicide, but he couldn't do even that. He, of course, once took eleven Adedrin pills at night but then automatically woke up at nine in the morning. The thing was that he had got used to taking sleeping pills even before Sarla's wedding—sometimes three pills, sometimes two. If Sarla got angry, sometimes he would even take four pills together.

He didn't like any other scientific or religious method of committing suicide. In the Japanese system of hara-kiri, people commit suicide by inserting bamboo knives into their stomachs. American citizens usually prefer jumping off the Empire State or the United Nations building. Ramnath thinks it's disgusting and painful to die from being crushed by traffic or jumping off a tall bridge into a river or by lying in front of a moving train. Last year, one of Ramnath's friends' wives had died by wrapping both hot and cold naked electric wires around her arms and waist. The news had terrified Ramnath so much that he didn't even go to his unfortunate friend's house for the funeral. He couldn't bear to see the dismembered, perverted state of any human body. As a child, after seeing a dog crushed by a truck, he had yelped *kain-kain-kain, kain-kain-kain* like a dying dog.

Sarla had warned him that he should soon make her Sarla Rastogi from Sarla Mathur, otherwise she would go mad or die by jumping into the Ganges. Ramnath had felt a similar terror at the time, he had wanted once again to yelp like a dying dog.

High-class people standing on the roof of the double-storied steamer were now waving their handkerchiefs. The noise of travellers and porters on the port. Calls of unknown names. The husky voice of the announcer on the loudspeaker says—This steamer is arriving from Pahleja port. In two minutes, the steamer will halt at the jetty. It's going to be exactly 6 p.m. Travellers going to Pahleja, Sonpur, Chapra, Muzaffarpur should buy their tickets. This steamer will open at 7.55 p.m. for Pahleja port.

Ramnath is not listening to anything. He cannot understand anything. His eyes are open. He is seeing. He can only see. He cannot do anything else. He won't listen. He won't feel the scent. He won't even be able to touch. He will only see, like people see hills, forests, dark caves and snakes in dreams.

Mahtab Ali, filled with happiness, pointed—Look, near the railing, wearing a white saree . . . Look, Sarla is standing there.

But Ramnath didn't listen. He had already seen Sarla. She was slowly getting closer and closer. Slowly, she was getting bigger and bigger, more and more beautiful, more and more upright. Kamlesh said, But why is she alone? Where is Kapoor-sahib?

By now, Sarla had also seen the people standing on the restaurant balcony. Perhaps she didn't have a handkerchief. She was waving her colourful umbrella. Her face started glowing with happiness. Kamlesh gestured that they had recognized her. She started laughing. Laughing, she started to descend from the steamer's bright stairs. Her porter, carrying a big holdall and a big attaché case, walked in front of her.

—But where is Kapoor-sahib?—Kamlesh asked again.

Sarla is returning from her marital home for the first time. Her gentleman husband should certainly be with her. Ramnath asked anxiously—Why Kamlesh? Won't you come down? She must have arrived at the gate. Why are you standing here now?

—Why are you screaming? Let's sit inside. Sarla will come here—Kamlesh answered succinctly and started lighting a cigarette. The matchstick extinguishes repeatedly in the wind. It will be dark in some time. The steamer will start shimmering with electric lights. Their reflections will create hazy images on the surface of the water. Sarla's eyes glimmer. What is she so happy about? Because Ramnath has come to the port? She should be sad about Ramnath—a sadness filled with sympathy. Especially in this situation, where Sarla herself has let down the radio station's Sinbad the Sailor.

It was the play *Sinbad the Sailor* that had turned Ramnath Rastogi's game—due to a slight mistake on his part. He had produced the play for All India Radio. He had also presented the play on the stage for an invited audience. It was only reasonable that Sarla play the heroine. Ramnath had given her the role of Basra's princess. However, after two rehearsals, Sarla caught a cold. Her voice became husky, started cracking into pieces on the mic.

ASD took Ramnath aside and said—Give her role to Mrs Dhanvantari. Sarla won't be able to do it. Your reputation will be marred. Officers from the department in Delhi are coming. They will form a bad opinion of you. I have told Mrs Dhanvantari. She will come to you.

Ramnath thought that ASD's advice was sound. He gave the role to Mrs Dhanvantari. Mrs Dhanvantari insisted he come to her house for breakfast. Sometimes, the camel turns unexpectedly. The camel of Time doesn't know right from wrong. It does not possess a conscience. The human is a conscientious creature. However, perched atop this godly camel, crossing new and newer deserts and oases, sometimes he falls due to the camel's turn and then finds himself in a laughable situation. To escape this desert storm, with his camel, he will push his nose into a sandy cliff and do pranayam. When the cliff itself flies away in the storm, he too will start flying here and there, and then faint in fear of death. This is what happened to Sinbad also. The primeval eagles of the desert island were flying around with him clutched in their beaks.

The camel turned. Ramnath, with his play, sometimes flew around Mrs Dhanvantari and sometimes around Sarla. Sarla was deeply offended—You have insulted me in front of the entire world! Everyone knows you are my friend. But, instead of me, you gave the play contract to that married woman! Now how will I face the ASD and PEX . . . ? What did you say, I had a cold? What difference does a cold make? The cold would have disappeared after four vitamin C pills. But you had to present Dhanvantari as the Princess of Basra! Alas, you do not know what applause I command from the audience when I appear on stage with an Arab scarf and handkerchief tied on my head and an upturned veil! I had played the role of Princess of Arabia in Nalanda Kala Mandir's play *Victory of Love*. I won 24 gold medals and 11 silver trophies. But you have insulted me publicly, Mr Rastogi!—Sarla stomped her feet, expressing her anger to the very end and left his room.

After this, he was spotted a couple of times, after his duty, with Mrs Dhanvantari under the queue of shadowy trees on Sinha Library Road. Sarla didn't attend the play. She had already taken a casual leave. When Ramnath himself went to her house, she was in make-up, like the film heroines, wearing an expensive printed Chanderi saree, sitting with her family members, feeding big samosas to a stranger. Sarla's old father said to the man—Sarla has made these samosas herself. Our daughter Sarla is as good a cook as a singer!

Ramnath also received a samosa and a cup of tea. But no one introduced him to Shibbanlal Kapoor. There was no time for introductions. Upon Kapoor-sahib's repeated insistence, Sarla sat with the harmonium. There was no one to play the tabla. Ramnath could have played something for the beat but he was angry. Of course, Sarla Mathur sang 'The River of Silence Drowned in the Whirlpool'.

While singing the song, she forgot the last stanza. Ramnath remembered it.

My reflection in a man-sized mirror
Trembled, the sky rained new clouds.
One question undid all the bonds of body.
My coquettish heart turned into a temple!
The river of silence drowned in the whirlpool!
Like an entire epoch drowned in the whirlpool!

But he didn't remind her. Hiding the stanza of the river of silence in his heart, he silently went off to the radio station. He started preparing to present Mrs Dhanvantari as the Princess of Basra. After that, this background song kept playing in his mind forever like in the Hindi films—sometimes with the tanpura and theka, sometimes just with the harmonium. This song which he didn't write, which was by his friend Kamlesh, he was never to be freed of this song after the accident of *Sinbad the Sailor*. He didn't want to be freed. Neither did he seek any revenge.

Not for revenge, he had insisted his friends come with him here at this time because he didn't have the courage to face Sarla Kapoor alone. His mirrors still had the kohled stains of long, delicate fingers. The rainbow-coloured butterfly wings on the door. Cracked window glasses. Stains on glasses. There is no doubt that he had loved Sarla with the entire force of his dreams and desires. But love is nothing exceptional. The exceptional thing is whether as Sinbad, he can climb the mountain of diamonds and jewels. And if he can return from that mountain with the Princess of Basra to his city Jerusalem, Damascus or Kohkan. The exceptional thing is the return— the return with the princess.

After returning from the balcony to the restaurant table, and signalling the waiter to take his order, Kamlesh was also thinking about Sinbad the Sailor. The play's title was *The Thirteenth Voyage of Sinbad the Sailor*. He had gone to watch the play. He had even liked Mrs Dhanvantari. She wasn't heavy, wide and vulgar like the average officer-wives. She had preserved her personality. According to behavioural sciences, such women could spend their lives in only two places—one, where balloons are hanging off the roof, which they could burst, like firecrackers, one after another with their hairpins. Another, where there are no other animals, not even pets, only cats, who, whenever and wherever, would lick with their soft tongues sometimes soles, sometimes knees, sometimes thighs and, while licking the thighs, grow intoxicated and slowly fall asleep.

Like Mrs Dhanvantari, Saanvli is a seven-tongued cat. The only difference is that Kamlesh is scared of cats. In his childhood, he neither murdered any cat nor did any frightening cat scratch or bite him. Despite the absence of any psychological reason, he is scared of cats, and rumours. Kamlesh is a courageous man but he is deeply religious. Philosophers say that to obtain success in life and business, it's important to be god- and law-fearing. Kamlesh wanted success.

Sinbad the sailor, cats, play, Sarla Mathur, Ramnath, Mahtab's sister-in-law Salma, Samresh, Mrs Dhanvantari, the restaurant of the steamer port, dogs crushed by trucks, schoolteacher Daya Ben, the song of the river of silence, and Saanvli—all these names are tied together like playing cards in a single packet and lying in front of Kamlesh on the restaurant table. If he wants, he can pick any card and turn it into a trump card. Like Duryodhan, the man drowning under the blue surface of the water should get the privilege of playing a trump card to save his own life.

He could pick any card he wanted. His name is Kamlesh. He is the sharpest journalist in the city. A female deputy-minister takes him away into her long car. After six months or a year, he will go on a tour of Europe's socialist countries as part of a government goodwill mission. He is not old. In front of his eyes stand horses of desires and aspirations, their saddles drawn tight. All he has to do is jump onto a well-bred horse. A racehorse. An Airavata emerging from the Churning of the Ocean. A horse that will climb the Qutub Minar. All the horses are standing with their heads held high, taut, chomping on their bits, waiting.

But Kamlesh closes his eyes. Turns his face. Touches the fresh teapot to check how hot the water is. Kamlesh is silent. Mahtab Ali is looking at the restaurant entrance and smiling. Ramnath stands up. Parting the curtain of the door, Mrs Sarla Kapoor arrived, she absolutely arrived.

—I knew it, Kamlesh, I knew that you would certainly come. That's why I had written to Ramnath-ji, asking him to tell you the date of my arrival . . . Good, Mahtab, that you have come too. Tell me, how is your wife? You do know that she was my classmate . . . ? Well . . . I won't take tea. I am very thirsty. Order a Coca-Cola or ginger ale for me—Sarla said so much, in different accents, with different gestures, but in a single breath.

She sat in an empty chair next to Kamlesh. Sarla has put on some weight. Layers of butter and sugar are settling on the face. Mahtab Ali asked—Where is your luggage? And your husband?

—I have sent the holdall and the suitcase to the bungalow with the servant. He didn't come with me. I came alone. I will have to return after a week. He is alone and, you know, married men shouldn't be left alone. He turns into the hero of *The Seven Year Itch* and starts eating next door—Sarla says and starts laughing rather anxiously. She looks at Kamlesh with a look of sweet, smouldering, slow flame of coals.

Ramnath felt the fire as well as Sarla's callousness towards him. Some time has passed, but she hasn't even asked if he is OK. Sarla is saying to Mahtab Ali—See, Mahtab-bhaijaan, I had promised you that I would buy an insurance policy from you after my wedding! I had promised, no? So, now, get me a multipurpose policy worth 20,000 rupees on any day you want. But yes, you have to throw us a beer party from the commission you earn!

Sarla has turned into an officer-wife. She has started drinking beers and ciders at parties. After every half-a-minute, she straightens the silken floral corner of her saree. She keeps babbling on. At times, her lips swell, at times they shrink into a circle, sometimes they become a parrot's beak, but her conversation never ends. Not even after finishing her Coca-Cola.

Ramnath was about to cry. To hide his teary eyes, he lowered his face. He picked up the menu card from the table and started reading the names of ice creams and bottled sherbets. It was as if Sarla hadn't even noticed him. As if Ramnath weren't even there. Even if he were there, it was as if he were a dateless calendar pointlessly hung on a wall to cover an empty spot. Ramnath was reminded of that dog of his childhood, who had been driven mad by the stone pelting of the colony's children, and then, bored of his life's routine, had committed suicide, screaming out his tale under a big truck carrying 10,000 smuggled sacks of rice. Ramnath wants to tell his tale to this officer-wife, but how?

His lips are sown shut like sacks of rice. His sunken eyes are damp. The background music of *Sinbad the Sailor* is echoing in his mind. Sarla Kapoor, leaning towards Kamlesh, the colour and inebriation of Coca-Cola dissolved in her eyes, was saying—Look, Kamlesh, I have come to Patna especially to meet you. It's a very important and private matter. You meet me alone tomorrow. Do one thing, come to my house, then we will go somewhere together. It has been so long since I have been to Kwality! The thing is that it's impossible to get out anywhere in Darbhanga and Muzaffarpur. And go where? It's a rural area. If I leave the house wearing a sleeveless blouse, the boys in the bazaar start whistling, their fingers pressed under their lips. It seems they will chew my naked arms.

And she laughed. The same expression of staring into the eyes, the same shyness, the same constant straightening of the saree's corner. The volcano of Pompeii started erupting in every part of Ramnath's body. He stood up and went straight to the counter. He paid for everything, tea, cigarette, coffee, Coca-Cola and then, without looking at them even once, left the restaurant through the curtained door. Kamlesh was silent.

Mahtab Ali understood. He understood that Sarla had consciously and with great planning, insulted Ramnath.

After Ramnath's departure, Sarla asked Mahtab very innocently, Our Ramnath-ji, does he still do the *Sinbad the Sailor* play for All India Radio?'

Mahtab Ali was Ramnath Rastogi's friend and companion under any circumstance. He felt great sympathy towards him. He had started thinking of Sarla as unfaithful. He had begun to hate her to a certain extent. He picked up the round cap from the table and put it on. He furrowed his brows. Kamlesh was looking at him. He knows that now Mahtab Ali will say something harsh. Something so harsh, so piercing that Sarla will turn cold like ice, and flat and even, like a cement floor. To change the subject, he asked Sarla, First I should know what's the matter! If it's something I can help you with, of course I will. But you do know what an ordinary man I am! What power do I have!

Sarla started smiling at the knight's move—Kamlesh wants to put this off. I hope I am not hurrying? Kamlesh is not a shallow man. The roots of his brain go deep into the ground. When I was in the radio, every man who came close to me, officer, artist, expressed interest in me in some or other way but not Kamlesh. Even after meeting me, his eyes didn't sparkle with hope or desire.

Even now, while asking this question, the eyes of this man were cold and innocent like a dead fish. Sarla Kapoor felt terrified at that instant by the silence and absence of warmth in Kamlesh's eyes. He asked again—The Assembly is open these days. I have to run behind ministers constantly. Tell me what needs to be done. Let me see if it can be done.

Sarla became terrified by this question asked in a straight and clear voice. She stood up and straightened the wrinkles of white silk. Then she sat taut, upright. Kamlesh waited for her to speak.

She remained silent for some time and thought about many things. If this has the opposite effect on Kamlesh, if he publishes everything in his newspaper, then the story of her life would be over! But when Kamlesh is asking with such interest, then he must be told at least something. What kind of a man is Mahtab Ali? He also has many high contacts in the government. Maybe some help can be arranged.

After thinking about everything, she said in a faint voice, The thing is, there is a government inquiry against my husband . . . he has been charged with taking a bribe of five lakh rupees from Jamnadas Gangaram Company. The Commissioner has been given the charge of the inquiry. Kapoor-sahib, my husband . . . you have met him already . . . has gotten to know that your minister is close with the Commissioner-sahib. This is the thing, Kamlesh! Now only you guys can save our lives. You are there, our Mahtab is there, find a way somehow. This is why I have come here. I will stay for as long as you want. If you want, I will go to your minister . . .

Kamlesh drowned in deep thought. The minister whose newspaper he edits has great respect for him, this is true, Commissioner-sahib cannot refuse him. But is it certain that he will really help Mrs Sarla Kapoor who has come here totally prepared to help her husband?

He said, Sarla-ji, come to my office tomorrow at around 6 p.m. We will decide what needs to be done. And saying this, he stood up.

Mahtab Ali had been sitting silently until then. Getting ready to leave, he said, Kamlesh, drop Sarla-ji to her house. I am going to Ramnath's. Who knows how many sleeping pills he might take tonight!—Sarla couldn't understand if Mahtab Ali's voice had sarcasm or sympathy or a slight loathing.

Kamlesh knows Mahtab Ali intimately, so he immediately understood. He said calmly to Mahtab Ali—Don't worry about Ramnath! Sarla doesn't want to break his heart. Today she was busy composing herself. Ramnath himself should have asked after her. After all, both of them have pride and ego. Anyway, send Ramnath to me in the morning. Sarla has only got married, she hasn't been imprisoned in a pyramid! She will meet Ramnath. Just like before. He doesn't want anything more anyway. He has always only been a lover, never been a buyer! Isn't that so, Sarla?

Sarla, smiling artfully, lowered her blushing face. Kamlesh had never been able to say so many things so clearly in his life before. He didn't hesitate to call Ramnath a lover, not a buyer in front of Sarla. He didn't tone down his voice. In the same tone, Sarla replied, I have no complaints with Ramnath. On the contrary, I have hurt him. But Kamlesh, he has to take the initiative. How could have I said to him: let's go, let's hire a boat tomorrow evening and go around the Ganges? Whatever it is, I do have the right to be shy.

Kamlesh started laughing, so loudly that people at the other tables began to look at him. Then he guffawed, patted Mahtab Ali's back like a tabla and said, Let's go, friend, today's theatre ends here!

After dropping Sarla home, he kept on the same rickshaw and roamed around like a vagabond till 11/11.30, 12/12.15, here and there, at times stopping to eat a paan, at times to see the posters and show cards of cinemas. When he felt tired and hungry, Kamlesh finally returned home.

His bedroom door was open. But there was no light inside. The light was coming from Gauri's room. Outside in the courtyard, the sounds, rising and falling, of Samresh's snores. His snores are very loud. Kamlesh has never returned home this late. He is hungry. He wants to forget the entire episode of the steamer port. Now no more, enough is enough. Horses with tightened saddles are standing, chomping on their bits. There are playing cards on the table. Which card should he turn into a trump card!

Saanvli, his maid, is sprawled on his bed. Maybe she is scared after a nightmare. She has folded her limbs. Like Henry Moore's famous statue, *Reclining Female*, Saanvli resembles a primitive animal.

Kamlesh took off his bush shirt and sat in a chair under the fan. He was drying off his sweat. The June of 1965 had not yet passed. It had been many years since such beautiful summer nights had been felt. He didn't switch on the light. For a long time, he sat silently in his chair. Sarla Kapoor, at any cost, will save her husband from the crime of taking a bribe. She is a clever woman. Ramnath will keep going to the radio station, produce play upon play. Our country has become progressive in every direction. Plans are made. New cities with factories and tall offices are made. Man is not like he was before. His clothes as well as the piece of flesh hidden inside have changed.

Kamlesh smiled and bolted the door from the inside. He is frightened of cats and rumours. He is god-fearing, that's why.

WARRIORS DON'T WORRY
ABOUT THE RIGHT TIME

The lantern dangling from the eaves in the corner of the veranda will soon extinguish. Uncle, sitting on a low stool, is looking towards the well. Engrossed. There is no oil, the wick has burnt off. The flame is dying. A huge well. A Spanish cherry tree stands close by. Filled with flower buds. Who is drawing up water in this dark? Who is it? Who are you? Someone will keep drawing water all night, by dawn the well will dry out. In the morning, people will say—Oh god, the well has dried up! Their eyes will bulge in astonishment. Not water, in the morning from the well will emerge mud, a number of dead frogs, a single mug made of peepal. A few broken bangles. A slate. A shard of broken pitcher. Two glasses. Five bowls. Like from the Churning of the Ocean emerged Airavata, Bhurishravas and a pot of venom. But Lakshmi won't emerge. But water won't emerge.

It's laughable to think about one's own thoughts. I had a drink of bhang before sunset. The spell hasn't broken yet. How late is it? Sunra hasn't come to call me. When will he come?

Who is in the well? Uncle asked affectionately. There is no answer. On the well, there is darkness, the west wind, two buried bamboos, a small bucket to draw up water and a Spanish cherry tree, no person. I said—Uncle! You're high on bhang, there's no one in the well. Uncle! What happened at court? Did you get finally a date?

Uncle closed his eyes. Remained silent for a long time. Then said—Your Aunt was in the well. She comes exactly at this hour to draw water. She comes straight from Shiva's planet. From the Kailasa mountain. Mahadev Bholenath says—Bring a bucket of water—and your aunt picks up a bucket and comes straight to this well. Exactly at this hour. Draws water in this dark.

It's been eight months since Aunt passed away. It was malaria. Turned into typhoid. She died. Childless. Desire disappeared with her. Aunt made many attempts at getting Uncle married to her younger sister. I couldn't have a child, I'll consider my sister's child as my own. Shanti had visited her elder sister's house many times. As pure and beautiful as a frangipani bud. I really liked her. But then I was worried, what if Uncle gets married to his sister-in-law? Aunt really tried. Shanti, make tea for him. Shanti, grind bhang for him. Listen Shanti, don't be shy, you're his sister-in-law. Then one day, Uncle once suddenly announced—You from Sonpatti, write to your mother. I've fixed something for Shanti. The boy has a BA, has a job in Patna. Won't take any dowry.

Shanti got married. Uncle kept drinking bhang and battling court cases with the extended family. Twice a week, he visits Purnea Court. Does his shopping in Katihar. Aunt died without a child. Uncle spends his time on the veranda, and in the evening, after drinking bhang, reflects on what has and what has not happened. There is no worry about the present. There is no hope or wish to turn or shape the present according to one's own will. Stories and tales about what has passed please the mind. What has passed was better, appropriate, preferable. And by thinking about what has not passed, the present remains forgotten and lost.

Listen, Kamal, let me tell you a tale. Once there was a great learned man in a village. He had memorized the whole Mahabharata and all the Puranas. He accumulated a lot of wealth by telling those religious tales. He didn't purchase a lot of land but buried sack after sack of real silver in the ground. After that, he died. He left behind a Brahman widow, three unmarried daughters, two little sons. The Brahman woman went to Kashi. The sons ran away to Calcutta or Morang. The silver coins remained buried in the ground. And three unmarried daughters. You are educated. Now tell me what happened to those three sisters! Who made it?'

Uncle tells the tale by the extinguishing light of the lantern. Not a tale, a true story. My aunt had two sisters. They were destroyed after the death of their father. The eldest sister Shobha went mad. She somehow got married, now she is a widow. Spends her days in her maternal home. The middle sister Vibha became my aunt. Shanti is in Patna, with her husband. Three tales of three sisters. Three rivers, thirteen streams. One river dried. The second also dried. The third is flooding. What flood?

Who is standing at the well?

Sunra arrived. Said—Dinner is ready. Your uncle is already invited. Astrologer-uncle has come for a discussion.

Yes, I am invited. We will have to eat curd and puffed rice. I will fall ill. I will die. But Astrologer-uncle won't listen to me. Uncle stood up while placing tobacco under his tongue and picked up a silk sheet from the clothesline, wrapped it around his shoulders. I followed Sunra into the courtyard. Four rooms in a row. A huge courtyard. A boundary wall. Damaged in some places. A garden on one side. Trees of lemon, guava, custard apple and night jasmine. Such a big courtyard, empty. Making a *bhaaaan-bhaaaan* sound. My maternal aunt is placing a plate on the veranda. Widowed as a child, my aunt spent all her days in her maternal home. She kept busy in the kitchen. Cooking for the farm workers. Boiling grains. Pounding puffed rice. She never observed any religious rituals. Never went on the Baidyanath pilgrimage. Never listened to the Puranas. Always surrounded by the prohibitory boundary of home and family. Married at a young age. Never went to her marital home. All her life, she remained how she was. But she doesn't feel any sorrow, any internal agony. Holding the weight of an unmoving body in her eyes, containing her heart within the borders of her white saree, she always keeps busy.

She remains entangled with her chores, in the kitchen, words from some song on her lips. She remains so entangled that she has no time for any worry.

Sunra asked—Sir, do you believe in ghosts and spirits? Today, in the evening, Madhusudhan-babu saw a ghost near the big peepal tree. He has fallen ill. Keeps crying out. The big peepal is an abode of ghosts these days. Every night, witches from the entire village go there to worship.

Listening to Sunra, my maternal aunt started laughing. Pouring ghee onto her plate, she said—Why go all the way to the big peepal? Ghosts live on our veranda, inside the well. When Brother sits on the veranda after drinking bhang, he sees someone drawing water. If not anyone else, my sister-in-law.

Aunt, my uncle is not a drug addict. Do not jest with him. It's not even been a year since Aunt died—I said. But the laughter of my maternal aunt is illuminating the entire courtyard and veranda. A red-green light. A rainbow. A tree of Spanish cherry in an arid compound. A song in the dark. My maternal aunt said—You, Kamal-babu, do not believe in ghosts and spirits. But I have seen sister-in-law at the well a few times. Wearing a bright saree, standing at the well, drawing buckets of water.

And after a long break, the same laughter. The same light. The same Spanish cherry. My maternal aunt goes on—Oh! One night it could have been a disaster. I was very thirsty. I woke up. There wasn't a drop of water in the pitcher. What could I do, I had to go to the well with a mug. Filled water. The night was dark. It was scary. It was then that Brother shouted from the veranda—Who is at the well? Who are you?—And as soon as he said it, he got up and started walking towards the well. But it was dark everywhere. I hid in the dark, then ran to the courtyard.

It means that Uncle has been seeing Aunt at the well since that night, isn't it, Auntie?—I asked. Aunt blushed. Aunt asked Sunra—You're still here? Won't you prepare the betel leaf for Kamal-babu?

Damn, I forgot—Sunra said and left. Aunt was reassured. She said while serving us curd—We are all a kind of ghost, Kamal-babu.

Warriors don't worry about the right time.

The night passed. The birds started twittering. Uncle and I are sleeping on the veranda. Sunra brings two glasses of tea—Sir, wake up, tea!

Drinking tea, Uncle asks—When does your college reopen? I was thinking of going to Jagannathpuri. Gayatri will also do her pilgrimage. She has never observed anything religious. I am not keeping well either. I can't sleep at night. It seems your aunt is calling me. I feel scared. I want to do the Jagannath pilgrimage once. What do you think?

What can I think? Gayatri-aunt will travel outside the village for the first time. Attend a pilgrimage. Her soul will find peace after seeing the gods. You will also get a break from court cases, farming, nightmares—I said in a peaceful tone. Uncle kept drinking his tea. He kept looking towards the Spanish cherry tree near the well.

Now the veranda is sunlit. I am drinking tea and counting the remaining days of my holidays in my head. When I come to my mother's maternal home during the holidays, I find peace in Uncle's love and Gayatri-aunt's affection. When Aunt was alive, I used to find even more happiness and peace.

But now there will be no peace. Neither by coming to the maternal house, nor by leaving it. Why not?

SNAKES OF SILENT VALLEYS

It was your last Calcutta night, and so many memorable symbols were being erected in your mind. Flowers on shrines, endless peace, dead trees, innumerable boats covering the nudity of the Hooghly—Belur on this side, Dakshineshwar on the other—fish (or snakes?) on the water's surface? You were in Calcutta for only a night, and yet I was indifferent, unavailable, lifeless—perhaps you were thinking this. Because it's not possible for you to think anything beyond this. The fault is not yours but of those expressions that have been wrapped around you like Pashmina shawls. These are not even expressions, only hollow styles through which you have learnt to see, speak and understand. The fish are still swimming in the currents of water, Anima-didi! But they are real fish, not colourful ones painted with Pelikan watercolours on expensive art paper. And your eyes cannot truly distinguish between the two any more. I am witness to that.

The Queen of Sheba gave two roses to Solomon. I couldn't offer you even two fish on Solomon's behalf. I couldn't ask you which one was real and which one I had bought from a Japanese art emporium. I knew that you weren't the Queen of Sheba, but a worthless sculptor's even more worthless nude sculpture, which the wise have tried in vain to cover up with a nylon saree and blouse.

Even I had tried to envelop myself in the deep valleys of darkness. Like one of the heroes of Sarat Chattopadhyay's stories, I woke up early one morning and went to Burma by ship. I had no other way to escape light, because light was as false as the bestial romanticism of darkness, because you were light, and Shyamal and Shashvatiya. It meant that light was a circle, and I had never liked being in the centre. Hence the stable business expansion of Rangoon women, hence the helpless penury of Manila women, hence the involuntary free-will of Hong Kong women, the impure modesty of Bangkok women, the democratic morals of Japanese women. I still remember a geisha from Tokyo, Anima-didi, because that geisha was you. Ever since this new democracy has been established in Japan, the business of the geisha has declined. This is why this woman studied sociology and history in university during the day and walked dimly lit streets at night. This woman, who was less a woman and more a girl and who had started wearing shorts instead of a kimono, had a very long name; but American soldiers in the evening pubs simply called her 'Kin'. When I called her Kin, the smile on her red lips widened.

'Indian?' Kin asked respectfully, and for the first time in my life I felt proud of my country's name. Then, bursting with pride, I ordered a third whisky, I had already become quite young, and the next day you and I had our ISC exams, Aunt had gone to bed, leaving us behind in the study, our old and sick Alsatian dog was growling outside on the veranda, and with your hands on my shoulders, you were saying, 'Khaggu dear, just go to Shyamal's bungalow. I've left behind my chemistry book.'

If someone else ever calls me Khaggu instead of Khagen I get livid and, at 11.30 at night, on the road of barking dogs, end up running a couple of kilometres. I'm about 15–16 years old, and, on solitary and abandoned streets, I like to run like the sound and return like an echo, because you are the broadcaster of sound—5 or 6 years older than me, my aunt's only daughter and you knit sweaters and gloves for me. I don't have a mother, not even a father. Father is no more, he had cancer. Mother is no more because I don't know where Mother is. I am here, money received from Life Insurance is here, Aunt is here, and you who knit sweaters for me.

Dogs bark on Elphinstone Road, people sitting at paan–cigarette kiosks throw flowers of film songs on returning prostitutes, cars halt under the shadow of Mahatma Gandhi Park, and false sobs and false laughs keep making my nerves quiver. The light is on in Shyamal Patnaik's study. I jump up to the window, press my face against its bars and ask—'Didi's chemistry book . . . '

Shyamal smiles a Flash player's smile on receiving a trail of aces. 'These are three aces, only three aces, but the entire world's wealth can be packed on these!' Sarkar used to say, very determinedly. Shyamal smiles because he possesses a trail of aces. After handing the book to me, he says, 'Wait, Khagen, let me drop you home by motorcycle.'

You get third division in ISC and start studying BA with sociology and history. Shyamal fails in BSc and enrols himself in BA with philosophy and mathematics. And I, standing alone in a BSc Physics laboratory, think that my existence is nothing more than an empty test tube. For years, I remained an empty test tube because I was indifferent, unavailable, lifeless. The grotesque odour of acids and gases crawling on every part of my body. I was silent. I was morose. *I* was not, because I did not possess any word to prove my existence. Life was not. Was not. Was not. There was only a huge Dahlia flower, and I was busy and lost in burning it with nitric acid.

Aunt is in the kitchen and we, meaning you and I, are sitting in the dining room facing each other. Above you is a huge picture of Vivekananda and I am staring at the picture, I don't have any courage left to stare below.

'How did your hand get burnt?'

'In the laboratory . . . '

'You return late every day these days!'

'Yes.'

'You study in the library?'

'Yes?'

'Then!'

'I go to Freemen's.'

You don't ask any follow-up question, because Freemen's is the purest bar of the city, where kimono-clad Iranian women dance the butterfly dance, and Anglo-Burmese girls perform striptease and Hindustani girls narrate the tales of Bengal's Rani Rashmoni to soldiers and sailors.

You have understood that time has not allowed me to stay the Khaggu that runs like the sound and returns like an echo. You have understood, and your hands unconsciously pull up the corner of the saree rolled off on the arm of the chair, although my eyes do not dare sink below the blue-and-bluer veins visible under the transparent skin of your neck. It's raining outside and your face is turning warm and white like sharp sunlight.

'Khagen!'

I try to raise my lowered head. I feel as if both your legs are trembling under the table.

'Khagen!'

'Khagen, does Shashvatiya go to Freemen's?'

'Often! Why?'

'Does she go alone? Or . . . '

'Why? Shouldn't one go with someone? Or is it only that one should not go with Shyamal Patnaik?' The tube bursts due to extreme heat and sharp shards of glass pierce your body and face. In your eyes, in place of beauty, nakedness appears, stains of blood appear, darkness appears. You push back the chair and you are screaming, 'You don't have any right to humiliate me, Khaggu! I know what you want from me. I have known it for a long time . . . you want me.'

You don't pause, you are going on, and Aunt is standing at the door, holding a plate. You are shaking like a delicate eucalyptus stem and I am smiling, drowned in my chair. When you are angry, you speak only English and I like it when you speak English—because then you don't resemble my aunt's daughter, you don't resemble my Anima-didi, you resemble that Anglo-Indian receptionist at Freemen's who gets angry when anyone misbehaves, but people don't mind, because they know that jazz, a glass of beer or rum or whisky or sherry and the chorus of strutting feet on a wooden floor possess the magical quality of ending anger.

'Anima, why are you abusing the boy? My Khagen is better than you at everything!' Aunt is kind to me because I've topped university, my picture's been published in *Swadesh Samachar*. Aunt is vexed with you because you write poetry in the style of Elizabeth Browning, and receive eight to ten letters every day. You stand up crushing the plates on the floor and straighten the corner of your saree fallen to the ground. The veins of your neck are tense, your breasts have hardened like balls of iron, your face is cracking. You run out of the room and then lean on the veranda railing, sobbing.

Shyamal . . . Shashvatiya Sarkar . . . Harshvardhan Sarkar . . . Freemen's . . . the three aces of the trail. Shashvati's older brother is my classmate and we both go to Freemen's. Shashvati also comes. Shyamal also comes. Only you never come, Anima-didi, only you; because those poems are floating in your mind, the ones Dante wrote for Beatrice, or Faust wrote for Helen. I feel like laughing after I drink the first glass of alcohol. You are writing a poem under the dim green light of an ace in your study. There is a naked woman, whom an erect python has constricted in its coils, and there is a green-coloured bulb in the open jaws of the python, light is spreading, you are writing a poem.

What will happen when the expansion of the line is complete?
The hubris of boundary will be crushed.
Only zero shall remain
Neither the hesitance of boundary
Nor the terrible union of lines' bond
Come, oh my Vast,
Let's break lines, unfinish boundaries . . .

Shashvati hands her used glass to Shyamal, and asks me, 'Now what's your plan, Khagen-babu? And what will Anima do?'

Shyamal purses his lips after pouring his drink down his throat. Anima . . . Shyamal's throat is scratching. Anima . . . As if Shyamal is a three-year-old child, screaming after falling off the swing. Anima . . . An old South Indian man has fallen off his chair, he is vomiting, the waiters are going to throw him out, he is screaming a girl's name who used to accompany him 40–50 years ago to the coconut fields to pluck fruit.

'Shashvat, I will go to London or New York. I love science. I like atoms more than humans. I find the free independence of electrons more beautiful than women. As a child, Anima-didi wanted to be Madame Curie, now perhaps she will become Dorothy Parker.'

Madame Curie . . . Dorothy Parker . . . Anima Chaudhary . . . these names cannot be lined up, didi, because you are a sadist. You derive pleasure from constantly piercing your body and soul with a blunt knife. Life in your room and life in Freemen's, they are so different! There is nothing alive here other than the present. Harshvardhan forgets that Shashvati is his own sister. Shyamal no longer remembers that doctors have forbidden him from drinking more than one peg. I cannot think anything, and it cannot happen that my mother suddenly emerges out of one of the Freemen's cabins, laughing, and says to me, 'You have grown up so much, Khagen!' This pub is an atmosphere, a song, an image—people lose themselves. You do not want to lose yourself. Whether it's a poem, or the nude woman of the ace, or a coiled python, you want to keep your existence alive and vocal under their shadows. What is human existence? An ample expression of their past and dreams! And what is your past? That book of chemistry, which you asked me to fetch from Shyamal Patnaik's house? What is your dream? You don't have any dream, didi, because you have to wander over mountains, rivers and snaked valleys for dreams. You hated wandering, you still hate it.

You remained in your study room, imprisoned and unconscious in the python's coils, you kept breaking and scattering. I was happy that you were melting, melting like an oozing wound.

'Anima is crazy,' Shashvati says and, in a mad frenzy, holds her arms behind her and stretches in an artful way. I know that she has learnt this style of stretching by watching one of Anita Ekberg's film 14 times. Like pigeons staring outside their lofts, her desire is eager to emerge from her body. Harshvardhan Sarkar, along with his chair, has gone to the other table where he is telling American jokes to the Navy boys.

'Shashvat dear, let's dance!' It doesn't cost Shyamal much to forget his existence in this ambience. The Freemen's orchestra is playing a fresh rock 'n' roll tune. Aunt has fallen asleep in the kitchen while waiting for me. Electron groups are circling the nucleus of the atom. They are waiting for the explosion, so that they can lose their existence. Shashvati smiles and blushes while looking at me. She has come to Freemen's with me and, of course, should dance only with me.

'OK'—I look at Shyamal and begin to laugh. He keeps staring at me like an idiot. I am now the only one, a full bottle of rum in front of me, and I am wondering if I can also douse the bottle along with the rum! I was contemplating, and there would have been no end to my contemplation had Kin not asked me, sitting in front of me, if I was Indian.

I had replied 'yes' and told her my name. I was very happy, and while ordering whisky for a third time, I told her that I liked her.

I liked Kin because she was just like you. Extremely beautiful, laconic, morose, and her eyes full of dreams. She had read the tale of Buddha and Vaishali's city-bride Ambapali in some book. She had heard the tale of Christ and Galilee's city-bride Mary Magdalene from a Catholic nun. Kin recited poems to me that she had published under a pseudonym in a university magazine. The gist of the poems was that she was in love with an unknown god of an unknown sphere, who would someday arrive in a boat of flowers and then, forgiving all her sins, take her to his goldsphere—where, sitting under a canopy of roses, he would watch the dance of his eternal beloved . . . It means that no woman wants anything more or less than a canopy of roses and a lover. This was not just Kin's dream, it was also yours. The only difference is that your mental frailty kept denying its own dream. Kin was a geisha, her parents had taught her to dance, sing and converse with men who spent coins. Kin was wise and talked to men. After the Great War, a new word entered Japan's dictionary—democracy. And Japanese girls began to hula-hoop on the streets. And Kin accepted new words in the same way that she accepted in her poems the unknown god of an unknown sphere.

New words, meaning candlelit pubs . . . the ink of silent streets . . . the odour of strangers' sweat . . . stains on beds in strange rooms . . . and hospital! In spite of being a patient of new words, Kin had never stopped dreaming even for a second. Walking swiftly alongside me on Old Palace Avenue Road, she said earnestly, 'I will receive my certificate after two years. I am very beautiful, and after looking at my picture in the university gown, thousands of boys will propose marriage to me. I will choose a suitable groom, I will get married, and in some small coastal town, I will build a new house behind which I will plant a huge rose garden.'

'Will you come to India, Kin? It was in my province that Buddha received enlightenment . . . ' Kin suddenly stops when I say this. She stands in front of me and searches for her dream in my eyes for a long time.

You don't have dreams, Anima-didi, so where would you search for them? You only possess the past, in whose dark valleys there is nothing but angry-enraged snakes . . .

I have returned from Freemen's at 1 a.m. and you have fallen asleep with your arms outstretched on the table. Asleep under the dim green light, you resemble a stream of the Yamuna. I have had a lot to drink and I want to swim in the icy coolness of that water.

Yes, desire is important but oh! my friend,
The night of union is not just a matter of our yearning.
—Faiz Ahmed Faiz

I do want to swim but my feet are enchained. I want to free myself. I want to liberate that naked woman who is constricted in the python's coils. Freedom . . . liberty . . . how dear, how complete these words are! But aren't these words impossible? We cannot break the chains on our feet because we do not know what was formed first, feet or chains. 'Water, water, every where, Nor any drop to drink.'—my father repeated these words by Coleridge whenever he was angry with my mother. I am intoxicated, and these words are now frozen on my lips. There is water everywhere, but not a drop to drink, not a drop, not a drop, not a drop.

It is past midnight, and you are lying below the ace like a broken ice sculpture. The front door is open. Wandering gusts of wind are making your hair tremble. I wonder: what if there were a blackout suddenly and darkness sprouted in the entire world?

Shashvati has said that Anima is crazy. Shashvati has said that Anima doesn't have any brains. I agree that Anima-didi doesn't have anything, not even a smile. But could Shashvatiya sleep so peacefully even in the unconscious haze of alcohol? I keep looking at your face drowned in sleep, didi, and I am reminded of oceans. Then I move very close to you and place my hands on your shoulders. I feel my hands are burning, that they are stuck to live electric wires. Your shoulders quiver and your body starts to shake like a drowning boat. At that moment, your eyes open. You look at me, you look at me with exhausted eyes and without removing my hands from your shoulders, you say, 'No, Khagen, no.'

Your look has exhaustion and helplessness but also peace. I remove my hands and you fall asleep on the table again. You fall asleep, and in the morning, Aunt says at tea, 'Anima's room was open last night . . . you would have had a problem if it were closed! I was awake—but what to do, I fell asleep in the kitchen! Hope you didn't have any problem, Khagen?'

I know who had a problem. And on that very day, I moved out into a hostel. Aunt started to cry. I felt sad, too. Only you neither laughed nor cried. In the taxi, I smile at you and a new wall of unrecognition springs up between you and me.

I didn't know then. I hadn't really recognized you then. I was an ordinary child who fetched you your chemistry book and to whom you seemed a princess from an *Alif Laila* tale. Now I know that you were helpless and wanted me to throw your helplessness out of the room, and bolt the door from the inside. You wanted this but you didn't know your own desire, your own dream. Every woman wants this. This is what she dreams. A canopy of roses and a prince arriving on a boat of flowers! No woman wants more or less than this. This was your dream too. But you were a widow's daughter, brought up hidden from the inauspiciousness of the world. You were suffering from an inferiority complex, you let Shyamal roam in pubs with Shashvati, you never told Khagen that you, too, wanted to come to Freemen's. Certainly, you wanted to come. You had a bank account, expensive jewellery and sarees, you were also beautiful. In Freemen's society, you would have become the atom's centre. The mere sight of you would have transformed professional alcoholics, they would have repented their old sins and declared that you are not a woman but a goddess descended from the skies . . . professional alcoholics meaning both Shyamal and I or either one of us.

Amar matha nato korey dao hey tomar charonodhular taley.
Sakol ahonkar hey amar dubao chokher jaley . . .

Make my head hang as low as the dust off your feet
And drown in my own tears all my vainglorious pride . . .

You had sung this song on the university's Foundation Day and my eyes had grown moist. I wanted you to say that your pride would drown in my tears. But you did not. You never said it, not even that night when I returned home absolutely drunk and scorched my hands on your shoulders. My hands are burning even now, Anima, because they have not left the support of your shoulders. You are not there, and there is an erupting volcano of memories, you are not there, and unknown snakes are crawling in the silent valleys of darkness . . . yellow snakes, on whose entire bodies dark blisters have sprouted. You are not there, and Shyamal and Shashvati have gone to Kashmir . . . Shashvati's elderly mother has gone mad, Harshvardhan spends all his days and nights at Freemen's. You are not and I am not . . .

When I told all this to Kin, she started wrapping and unwrapping her scarf with her fingers, then spoke after much thought. Whatever she told me in her American English, the gist of it was that you were waiting for me that night and you had opened the doors of not just your room but also your heart. I went mad. Really, I went mad. But now there is no way to come back from Tokyo. I didn't even know in which college of which city you'd become a lecturer.

Didi, there is a society around us, there are many societies in this one big society, like a magician pulls out a small box from the big box, an even smaller box from the small box, and finally from the smallest box emerges a small, lovely pigeon flapping its wings and perches on the magician's shoulder. But there is no room for air, water or light to enter the boxes we are imprisoned in. Our pigeons are dead, our shoulders carry their corpses. I have appointed Kin to wash off the stench of dead bodies from my body. When we were leaving Tokyo for India, she said to me that it's not like what happens on screen doesn't happen in real life. She said to me, 'Anima must be waiting for you.' Every woman waits. If not for men, for past memories. I couldn't believe it, because Kin was true, much truer than you. Her eyes may not have poetry but they had music. I have never refused the madness of music. She told me that she wouldn't be able to make me the boundary of her life. The habit or desire of drawing boundaries may exist in her dreams but not in her blood. I couldn't believe the force of blood.

We came to Calcutta and I started building a mihrab over myself. Kin said she would try to live, adjust herself to my situation. I withdrew the last rupee from my bank account and Kin became the owner of Japan Drying–Cleaning Centre on Park Street. She knew how to talk to men and the business started to flourish. I decided I would teach in a college and research nuclear physics. Kin would place a 5–10-rupee note in my pocket every evening so I could keep meeting people, and I kept meeting people . . . sometimes in a restaurant, mostly in pubs!

One day, I ran into Shashvatiya, Shyamal and Harshvarshan at Victoria Memorial. Shyamal was a barrister in the High Court; Shashvatiya was the wife of an even more successful barrister. Only Harshvardhan was where he had been, race horses were galloping on his tongue, his eyes had the same crimson circles. He took me to a corner and told me about you, Anima. It didn't make me sad. Now it will never make me sad. Why? You never seemed so helpless that one could feel bad for you. Actually, you always seemed so powerful and solid that one almost wanted to see you helpless, guilty and suffering. The other day, I had gone to your flat in Kamla Mansions to see you suffer. I asked Kin to come with me but she didn't. She said, 'Don't even take my name in front of her. She is in trouble, she must need you.'

It's night. I don't have the courage to see your face in daylight. You are sitting alone in the bedroom, there is a big table in the middle of the room, and only the top half of your body is visible. Someone I have not met before. An unknown face . . . an unknown face, not a face at all but a broken teacup, on the surface of which are many extinguished cigarette butts. You raise your eyes, look at me, smile and say

SNAKES OF SILENT VALLEYS

in a very sweet tone, 'It's been more than a year since your aunt passed away. She transferred the house in your name. She said you will live in that house once you get married.'

I knew that you could speak only like this. I have come to Kamla Mansion just to hear all this. It doesn't surprise me that there are morphine tablets on the table along with a glass of rum. Harshvardhan Sarkar has just told me that you are in the seventh or eighth month of pregnancy. I am not surprised by the rum bottle or the tablets or Aunt's death. Your saree is tied loosely. And your swollen stomach looks terrifying. Your face is dirty, and I glimpse Susan Hayward from the film *I Will Cry Tomorrow*. Didn't you ever try to jump off the eighth floor of Kamla Mansions? No, you must not have wanted to die, Anima-didi, because you are not sad even now. Aunt has left you money. And you can buy thousands of rum bottles. Why the sorrow then? Sorrow is an illusion, a mental perversion, a weakness of the soul . . .

'Khagen, should I bring you a glass? Or you don't drink rum?'

'I don't even drink beer.'

'That's good. Kids shouldn't drink. I drink. I am getting my child used to it from now.'

'Your child?'

'Yes, Khagen, yes! My child growing in my womb! I am getting it used to rum. Not even a drop of brandy, only rum! It makes you healthy. Are you seeing me? I am double than before.'

'It's possible that you are triple. But what difference does it make?'

'What difference does it make? Nothing makes any difference ever . . . You know, Khagen, I was a lecturer at Delhi University. International Book Trust had awarded their First Prize to my poems. My name began to be taken alongside Eliot and Pound. Then Mother died and I was left alone, absolutely alone . . . '

'There is no need to tell me.' I turn once again into the Khagen who hates you. Who has no sympathy for you, who has never had any sympathy for you.

Your fingers look like they are made from bamboo, there are dark stripes of thick veins running through them. There is a stench emanating from your body, like you have not touched water in years. Your lips are black, chapped. There is no table lamp in front of you, because you yourself are the naked woman and the python has entered your stomach.

'I will send my son to study in London, Khagen. There he will dance with white girls in clubs and write poetry.'

Poetry is not dead yet. Perhaps, poetry never dies! But what you said is not poetry but an indication of a situation when people find themselves incapable of making fun of anyone else but themselves. You have wrapped this cheap alcohol bottle, this cheap rented room and its miasma around your existence so that you can make fun of yourself.

I know, didi, how the map suddenly changed. Shyamal and Shashvatiya didn't change. They still stroll around the manmade lake in Victoria Memorial after stopping their car in the dark. But you? I feel that you have not changed. Only the map has changed. Inside, you are still the same, because you want to forget in this intoxication that there is darkness and there is nothing but darkness at night. You don't have the courage to lower your head and look at your enormously swollen stomach. When I was entering the room, you were startled and wanted to cover up your body with the wide corner of your saree. You thought if the corner of your saree turned into flames, you would stand engulfed in fire and say that you are Sita, sinless, it's not your fault . . .

'Do you remember that Tagore song, Khagen? Will you sing it right now?'

'Which song?'

'Any! Would you sing any song?'

'Why should I sing?'

'Just.'

'I won't sing.'

And you smile, as if blisters are growing on water, as if worms are crawling on damp earth. And slowly, the size of the worms increase and they turn into snakes, snakes emerging out of your lips, snakes emerging out of your breath! I cannot tolerate these snakes of perverted odours, I want to run away outside into the fresh air . . .

Only two things have happened: you are pregnant, you drink a lot and your solitary life, your introverted heart is still as it was. If you didn't have Aunt's bank account and cheque book, your solitary freedom couldn't have been maintained.

If you walked on the streets, dogs and wolves would have followed you, growling. If you would have been inside a room, the windows would have been cracked by bricks thrown at them, and a sound, a call, a forgotten song would have entered through that crack and shaken your entire existence. You have money and solitude, and you are committing suicide.

No, I do not want to die. I only want to kill the flame burning in my stomach. A wrong Jesus Christ is growing in my womb, I do not want to raise the child. And now the world doesn't even need Jesus Christ, it needs atom and hydrogen bombs!—You want to say it but you don't have the courage. You didn't go to the doctor at the beginning because you didn't have the courage, and the thing is that you had been dreaming all your life of a beautiful child. There was a picture of Vivekananda on the wall of your study and you were captivated by his big eyes and you wanted your son to possess similar eyes.

I don't know who the father is of your unborn child. Maybe you don't know either. When you fell asleep naked on the floor or on a table in a haze of dreams or whisky, you don't know who entered the room and who left. Whether you know or not, it doesn't matter—because you have turned violent. You want to kill Jesus Christ by crucifying him on the cross of alcohol bottles and this is your defeat. I am happy. I am very happy.

The bottle in front of you empties and you take out a new bottle of rum from the closet. Outside, it is raining and I don't want to go back drenched.

'Where are you staying?'

'I have taken a flat in Park Circus.'

'You are going to be here permanently?'

'I have to be.'

'You are alone?'

'No.'

You don't ask who is with me if I am not alone. You close your eyes and think for a minute. Who knows what you think.

Like Tennessee Williams' Mrs Stone, you don't know what to think and what to forget. You just want to escape. You are afflicted by the fear of the conclusions of your thoughts. You are unable to ask who is with me if I am not alone. It is raining outside and I don't want to get wet.

'Now you leave, Khagen.'

'Why?'

'You must be expected.'

End. This is all that I wanted to know. I wanted to know whether you would suffer if someone was waiting for me somewhere, meaning me, Khagen, who fetched chemistry books from Shyamal, who drank beer with Shashvati at Freemen's . . .

And Anima-didi?

When I returned to my flat, Kin was lying on the sofa, gazing at the roof. She looked at me and smiled, she said, 'Should I make some coffee? It seems you are very tired.'

'Yes.'

'Freshen up.'

'Let me drink coffee first.'

And when both of us talk and drink our coffee, and I tell her everything, she decides that Anima-didi should be brought here. I have no objections because I know that tomorrow when we—meaning, Kin and I—will go to your Kamla Mansions, a 'To Let' board will be hanging outside your flat.

SISTERS-IN-LAW

Padma arrived in the courtyard dismal and worried. There was a demure streak of guilt and regret in her eyes. Without saying anything to her sister-in-law, she entered the northern room. From the kitchen, her sister-in-law asked: 'Is it Laal-daai?'

Without answering, Padma came out of the room with a comb and a mirror and sat down on the mat, quite morose.

Ramganjwali came out of the kitchen, wiping her sweat-covered face with the corner of her saree, and was stunned by Padma's morose eyes, limp gestures and lowered forehead: 'You didn't get anything, not even a rupee?'

She moved closer and, caressing Padma's forehead affectionately, said, 'Why, dear? Why are you so sad? Didn't you meet the rascal?'

'No, Bhauji, it's not like that. I did meet the rascal, he even gave me 2 rupees, but a strange thing happened. Oh, a disaster, Bhauji! What can I say!' said Padma, licking her dry lips.

She untied two 1-rupee notes from the corner of her saree and handed them to her sister-in-law. Bhauji's worry dissipated: 'Whatever may happen, I have 2 rupees. Now what's the worry?'

Both Padma and her sister-in-law are widows. Padma is about 23–24, Ramganjwali is about 32–33. And both are childless, of independent disposition.

Padma's village Vangram is a huge village. There is a high school, police station, post office, hospital and market. This is why it's not difficult for these two Brahmin widows to live their life here. In a village of about 2,000, at least 200 are rascals.

However, tonight Padma was sad. Her sister-in-law asked again, 'Lal-daai! You're behaving like a child. It can't go on like this. Tell me what has happened. Did the police detain you on the streets? These days, the policemen roam the woods all night.'

'Which constable would dare to detain me? Does the inspector not know me? I don't know how to tell you what has happened, Bhauji! Just assume that I am not alive—I have died.'

Bhauji laughed, 'OK, I have accepted that you are dead. But tell me who killed you, how did you die?'

Then Padma began the tale of her night—

'I ran into the rascal near the temple. I took him behind the temple and said: "Hey you, I need 5 rupees." He said: "You go to the haunted tree, I will bring the money." He didn't have the courage to do anything else in the temple. I was waiting for him under the white fig tree in the haunted area. He came after a long time. He placed 2 rupees inside my blouse and then, holding my hand, said, 'It's just 2 rupees. I'll give the other 3 rupees early in the morning.' And then he licked and kissed me for a long time. I was in a hurry, I worried that if I get too late, Bhauji would get mad, but he just wouldn't let me go. Sometimes he would take me in his arms, sometimes something else. Eventually, even I couldn't control myself and it felt like the entire tree had turned into a swing and I was flying in the sky with that rascal.'

Suddenly the Ramganjwali pressed Padma's hands forcefully and said: 'Laal-daai, don't go into so much detail. Tell me, what happened next.'

Padma continued, 'Then the rascal undressed me. It was as if I was out of my mind. Right at that moment, a constable came along, humming loudly. As soon as the rascal saw the constable, he ran away, leaving me behind. I just couldn't take it. What a coward! I began to run behind him. But he disappeared into the dark woods. I tried looking for him, I couldn't find him anywhere. I called out his name a couple of times, but nothing. The constable had strolled off down another path and gone away. I was running from one tree to another. After a long time, the rascal screamed from somewhere: "Padma! Oh Padma! Come quickly." I ran towards the sound. I found the rascal lying naked under a tree, writhing, moaning. But, Bhauji, it was if I was high on bhang. Seeing his naked body, all his organs under the moonlight, I couldn't help myself. I didn't have an ounce of sense left, where was I, what was I doing, why was I doing so. What more can I say, Bhauji, I can't remember what happened after that. But when I came to, I saw that the rascal was no more, only his body lay on the ground.'

'Oh god!'—screamed the Ramganjwali.

'Bhauji, a snake had bitten the rascal,' screamed Padma. 'That's why he was calling out my name. Bhauji, I slept with a dead man, now how will I live?'

Padma started crying. She cried for a long time.

Then Bhauji said, 'Laal-daai, go, go take a bath in the pond and sprinkle some holy water from the Ganges. What else can you do? When there is no shame in sleeping with a living man, why feel shame in sleeping with a dead one?'

Padma got up and went to take a bath.

VENI SANHAR

Sita felt that she was watching a play where medieval bandits had tied a princess to a tree in a dense forest and the princess' helpless cry had set the forest ablaze.

Sita felt like a medieval princess. The robbers have run away leaving her tied to a tree and a horrific forest fire is fast approaching. The forest is burning. Screaming animals are running away in swift leaps. There is smoke, noise, darkness and the crimson flames of fire have centred Sita and are flying towards her from every direction.

She is tied to the trunk of a tree. The bond is very strong. She cannot untie herself despite wanting to. Unlike the animals, fearing for their lives, fleeing the forest, she cannot even try to run.

Sita lives in a high-school quarter near the forest. Today is Sunday. After her lunch, Sita likes to lie down on a palm-leaf mat in the half-light and half-shadow of the forest veranda and read yesterday's newspaper or drown herself in a light sleep.

The light sleep slowly turns deeper but not today. Not on a Sunday. Who knows when Triloknath might ask for something. When he might call out. When he might say: 'One mustn't sleep during the day, Sita! It's bad for one's health . . . wake up, come here.'

Sita hates hearing about her health. She can listen to anything. She can swallow Triloknath's every sermon. Just not that she is ill, that she should take care of her physical weakness. She wants to forget the illness. It's another thing that she cannot.

In a light and sweet sleep, Sita saw all of the Aambazaar forest on fire. The forest that extends from Jauli to Kodarma to Kodarma-Hazaribagh to southern Bihar. Forest; small cliffs and fields filled with mica mines; narrow, black roads like ribbons tied-entangled in thick buns of long hair; little tribal colonies on the sides of the hills; flat ground of red sand, red tiled roofs, houses of clay in a row; and this town Aambazaar; this small high school! Everything was burning, like raw mutton scorched in a cauldron, and now, finally, the fire has reached her quarter.

Sita felt that a big ball of fire has bounced in and exploded like a bomb near her feet. Sita screams awake. She escapes the boundary of her unripe sleep, she returns.

There was a huge hole in the tiled roof of the veranda, and hot rays of the afternoon sun, long-slanted stripes of heat, were frozen on her face. As soon as she opened her eyes, blisters of colour started floating across them. Red, blue, yellow, green. Her eyes began to water. She couldn't understand anything. Who was she, where had she come, where did the lava from the erupting volcano go?

She tried, in vain, to stand up in the morning. Her legs began to tremble. There is a rocky courtyard in the front, a courtyard of red sand on which shimmer minute fragments of mica. Surrounding the courtyard is a high and wide enclosure. Beyond it, green-green trees of papaya and bananas everywhere! Beyond the trees and field and school building, a hostel for tribal boys, a laboratory for the science department, and then the forest.

Slowly, the stains of colour started to disappear. Only one colour remained—brightness everywhere. Then, in that brightness, Sita wasn't sure when a small black stain sprouted. A black stain on the courtyard wall! It slowly began to spread and grow, it got uglier, and staring at the stain, Sita's heart began to drown in an unknown fear. As if she didn't have a heart but an unformed piece of stone which, broken after colliding with a hard rock, was now drowning in the black river of fear.

Trying to save herself from drowning, Sita felt that her mouth was filled with blood, that bloody foam was leaking from her lips. She tightened her jaws, bit her lip. Sita saw that a cat was sitting on the northern corner of the boundary wall. A black cat!

At first she thought it's not a cat but a female cheetah. But a cheetah is not this ugly, not this terrifying! It's is a wild cat. Mottled patches on a black body, as horrific as a bulldog. And a hideous face with red smouldering eyes.

Sita screamed again and started trembling like a patient of hysteria. Triloknath was busy calculating government grants inside the house. Dearness allowance for teachers: 3,000 rupees. Lab instruments for scientific studies: 5,000 rupees. Triloknath has been the headmaster of this school for the past 17 years. He saves the government grants for himself. He saves for himself the absence penalty that the boys pay.

Triloknath was busy with his accounts. He didn't hear Sita's scream, her fear or her fainting. He was thirsty. He called out to Kamala: 'Kamli, bring me a glass of water . . . and see what your madam is doing.'

Kamala is a tribal woman of the Munda caste, middle-aged. Her husband is the school's head gardener. Her oldest son studies in the 5th Standard. Kamala doesn't receive any salary from the headmaster. She gets two meals a day. Sometimes, Sita gives her an old saree. Nirmal sometimes calls her inside the room and gives her a couple of rupees. Kamala is not a servant and Kamala is totally a servant. Sita is usually ill. Vidyamayi doesn't want anything to do with household chores. This is why Kamala takes care of the household.

There is always a lot of trash in the courtyard. Muddy, dirty clothes hanging off the taps! Spiderwebs on the windows! But no one can be angry with Kamala. If someone says anything to her, she flares her wide nostrils and says, 'You, you can't do it? Am I your servant, who will cook, wash the dirty dishes? Do you pay me a salary? How much?'

Kamala was doing the dishes near the tap. At the back of the house, near the bathroom, there is a hand pump. Nirmal's window opens onto the pump. If he is in the room, he sits on the window and reads some book in the same unchanged position. He smokes a cigarette. He talks to Kamala while she fills water from the pump, does the dishes, bathes. This is his life's first and last pastime.

'Kamala, Father is asking for water.'

'So be it! I am scrubbing the dishes.'

'First go and give water to Father.'

'Won't go! Tell the daughter to give water to her father.'

'You're totally mad, Kamli!' said Nirmal and threw the stub of a cigarette at her. Kamala dodged it

She began to laugh. Kamala is a wild woman. She is now middle-aged but her body still has the tautness and swiftness of a young female cheetah. When she laughs, rows of white teeth shine among black gums and red lips. Triloknath called out again. Kamala, forgetting the cigarette-stub incident, begins to rinse a glass.

Nirmal remained standing near the window. He kept looking at the dirty dishes near the tap. Copper plates. A big vessel for cooking rice. Small china plates. On one plate lay a half-eaten head of fish. Vidya must have left it. She can't eat a fish head. But Kamala, away from the sight of Nirmal on the window, will chew the head. She'll keep scrubbing the dishes and chewing the head. The head, and the bones lying on other plates.

Suddenly, Nirmal heard Kamala scream: 'Babu! Come, Babu . . . Madam is having an attack!'

Nirmal heard her but didn't panic. He put on an undershirt and a pair of slippers, then came out of the room. The door opens onto Vidyamayi's room. Then, a long veranda. In one corner of the veranda lay his stepmother, Sita Devi, unconscious on a palm-leaf mat.

Without stopping, he went into his father's room. Triloknath, despite Kamala's screams, had not been distracted from his accounts. Nirmal stood there silently for some time. Then he said, 'At least take Ma to a doctor in Ranchi once . . . even last Wednesday . . . '

Nirmal pauses, for, lifting his eyes up from his papers, Father was looking towards him. Nirmal keeps still, keeps standing. Triloknath says, 'Sita is your mother (even if only a stepmother!). Take her to any doctor you want! Why are you asking me? What is the cure now?'

Triloknath had hoped that Sita would get better after becoming a mother. Everyone had hoped the same. But Sita didn't get better. There is a five-month-old child in her lap. When she is happy, Sita calls him Bablu! . . . Bablu! But during one of her episodes, she had thrown Bablu off the bed. The four- to five-month-old child was writhing on the red cement floor. The injury was to the head, where a lump had appeared at the back. Bablu didn't die, but he was unconscious. Sita, lying on the bed, kept going crazy with pain and anger. Why did she keep going crazy?

After the death of Nirmal and Vidyamayi's mother, Triloknath didn't have any wish to remarry. Nirmal was a sharp boy, Vidya pranced about like a bunny. Ten to twelve years had passed like this. It was then that Triloknath visited his village. Sita's widowed mother lived in the same village.

Just a few months after the wedding, Sita had contracted typhoid. Sita had almost died. Doctors from big hospitals in Hazaribagh, Ranchi and finally Patna saved her. She didn't die, she got better, but the terror that had emerged in her big eyes never disappeared. She gets agitated with everything. Shaking-trembling, she faints. She clenches her teeth, her lips become bloody. She starts laughing at anything. She rolls on the floor with laughter. She breaks anything that comes within the border of her limbs. She feels scared, screams in terror. When she regains consciousness, she stays sitting on the floor or on the chair, her limbs folded.

Silent, lost, trying to identify others with a bewildered gaze, searching for a path out of the darkness of the dense forest—Sita keeps wandering. The path is not found.

The path is not found, and trying to stand with the help of Kamala's strong arms, Sita starts screaming, 'Look there, Kamala, on the wall . . . she's still sitting. Look at that, my death is sitting . . . where is Babuji? Where is Babuji?'

Kamala saw. Nirmal came out of the room and saw. That black, terrifying, ugly cat was still sitting on the boundary wall. Looking at the veranda with wild eyes, the cat was neither growling nor moving from her place. Triloknath came outside, 'What is it? What is on the wall, Kamli?'

'It's a wildcat, Babuji! Madam is scared for no reason. Why fear it, it has come from the wild, it will return to the wild,' Kamala said, and seating Sita on a chair, went to chase the cat away. The cat didn't run away. Walking a slow and lazy walk, she came near the house, then leapt onto the veranda's tiled roof and perched there

Bablu sleeping in the cradle started crying. Triloknath went into his room. Kamala went to pick Bablu up but was surprised—Bablu's body was like a hot pan. Kamala placed Bablu in Sita's arms, who was sitting on the veranda, and went off to fetch a thermometer.

102-degree fever. However, Bablu is still drinking milk and smiling through his feverish haze. All the buttons of Sita's blouse have come undone. The wrinkled yellow skin of her stomach is visible. Vidyamayi is standing near Sita, caressing Bablu's head. Nirmal is strolling in the courtyard, smoking a cigarette.

Whenever Sita goes crazy, Nirmal is reminded of his mother. He was very young then. Very young. All the boys and teachers of the hostel had roamed around madly till midnight, with torches and petromax, through the forest surrounding Aambazaar. Nirmal's mother's corpse was found at 2 a.m. A pack of wild jackals, surrounding the body, were guarding it, and his rather heavy ma was lying in a shrub of Bengal currants as if she were sleeping inside the mosquito net at home.

Nirmal feels melancholy at the thought of his dead mother. He starts thinking about the other women of Aambazaar. Female cheetahs like Kamala. Nirmal likes thinking about women's bodies and women's habits. He couldn't study much. He now has a small shop of English medicine in the market and, sitting in the shop, he keeps thinking about his mother, about Sita Devi. Ill tribal women cannot pay the full price of medicines. The Christian nurse of the only doctor in the bazaar, Dr Ganguly, makes very dirty jokes. Why did Ma commit suicide? Why didn't Ma think that Nirmal was so young, Vidya was so young?

Suddenly Bablu's eyes open, he starts screaming. His face is swollen, it has turned red like a slice of watermelon. And Sita's lap is burning. Her thighs are burning. Sita felt that now, in an instant, Bablu will turn cold and his breath will stop forever. Sita was intoxicated, inebriated with her illness. With empty eyes, she looked at Nirmal and said, 'My Bablu is going, Nirmal.'

Nirmal thought: right at this moment Sita will fall to the floor with the child and, with flailing limbs, lose consciousness. He moved forward and snatched Bablu from her arms. Taking the towel off the clothes line, and wrapping Bablu with it, he told Kamala he was taking the child to Dr Ganguly, 'You and Vidya take care of younger Ma until then! I will be right back . . . '

Seeing the courtyard empty, the cat jumped off the roof and tiptoed into Triloknath and Sita's bedroom. Sita's eyes were open. She saw the cat go in. Sita writhed off the chair and went into the bedroom, 'I will kill it! . . . You don't understand . . . it's a spirit . . . that's not a cat, it's a ghost . . . it has come to eat my Bablu.'

She went inside and started peering under the bed. That black cat was crouching there, near the wall.

Sita threw a hockey stick at her with great force. The cat jumped to one corner. She didn't get scared or growl, she crawled away and began to understand Sita. The anger of the one who'd thrown the stick grew. She bolted all the doors from inside. Closed all the windows. In the bedroom, there was now almost complete darkness. From the small window high up on the wall, the ripe rays of a setting sun kept streaming in. Sita

105

picked up the paperweight from the table and aimed for the cat. The cat emerged from the under the bed, then jumped up onto the almirah. Sita reached under the bed and pulled out the hockey stick.

The room is closed. All the doors are closed. Kamala and Vidyamayi, standing outside on the veranda, are staring at each other. The cat, in an attempt to escape the room, is causing a ruckus. Triloknath is pacing in circles in his room. Nirmal is running towards Dr Ganguly. Five-month-old Bablu is unconscious in his arms.

Sita wants to catch the cat. She is intoxicated. She is mad. The sick Sita wants to kill the cat. What is this drama? This ugly cat, a mad woman and, in the next room, an old, fat man scared of himself?

The cat jumps. Sita picks up a big stone vase and hits the cat. The cat writhes and crawls up Sita's back and plucks the skin off Sita's neck. Sita turns. Lightning swift, she catches hold of the cat's neck. Pieces of the vase are buried in the cat's body. Squeezing the cat's neck with her hands, Sita laughs. A horrible laugh! A laugh of death!

Hearing the mad laugh, the black, ugly and frightening cat opens her crimson eyes. She stares at Sita.

Sita's mad laugh suddenly stops like a vinyl record paused. Sita is looking at the cat. The cat is looking at Sita. In Sita's eyes is madness, fire and the venom of death. But what is in the cat's eyes?

Sita stops. Sita stops like a suddenly stumbled child. What isn't in the cat's eyes? Sita's fingers tightening round the cat's neck pause. They grow loose. Sita's body, the veins in her neck, the tension in her chest break. She bends and places the cat on the floor like a china toy, and then opens the door.

Sita goes to Triloknath's room. The box of clothes is in that room. Sita strokes her back with her fingers and sees rusted brown blood. She takes off her blouse. She opens the box and starts looking for another blouse. Sita's mind has broken. Even the body is not intact. How has she become! Frozen, shrunken, how small, how frail she has become! Putting on a new blouse, she walks to her husband. Triloknath can't muster the courage to look at her, to keep looking at her. Sita is leaning against the back of a chair and looking at the picture on the wall.

In the royal gathering of Duryodhan, the image of Draupadi's disrobing. But Krishna is not present. Dushasana is pulling her saree. Everyone else is watching. The five Pandavas are standing with their heads lowered—only Krishna is not present. Sita, it seems is about to faint again.

'Even if Bablu dies, what will happen? You shouldn't go so crazy,' Triloknath was saying with his head lowered. His voice was echoing inside a mountainous cave. Sita turned around and saw Kamala and Vidyamayi standing on the veranda. She saw the half-dead cat crossing the veranda in a slow gait. Sita's veins tensed up.

With all her might, she grabbed her husband's neck and started screaming, 'You . . . you want that . . . you want Bablu to die? Die? You . . . '

Triloknath got up from the chair and pushed Sita away. Sita fell on the floor. Sita sprang back up like a wild cat. She saw Triloknath approaching, she screamed in fear and ran out of the room. Out of the room, out of the courtyard, out of the school compound.

First, there is a field. Then the forest and small cliffs shimmering with fragments of mica! From the corner of the forest, a slanted road of red sand goes towards the bazaar.

Sita is running alone through the forest. Suddenly she turns and sees—a black and ugly cat. An unknown cat, one she has never seen before, is following her.

LIKE A WALL OF GLASS

'Why do you like the colour blue so much? This deep-blue colour. Why do you like it? Are there no other colours left in the world? Vivid colours? Faint colours? Colours that swim through the eyes and spread as songs in the mind? But your blueness. Blue ocean and blue sky and blue fish and only blueness. Kapoor-sahib, is this not filth? The perverse tangles of your mind, your complexes, the false story of your entire life . . . what symbol of truth do you want to turn your blue colour into? A symbol of morbidity? A symbol of the acute macabre? . . . OK, not symbol, sign! Fine, I will call it a sign, but do you want to compose only signs of the macabre for us? . . .'

No, no! Satya didn't say so much. She said none of this. She had merely smiled with a slight boredom on her lips, and asked, 'Why do you like the colour blue so much?' Kapoor couldn't immediately think of an answer. In fact, he didn't expect this question from Mrs Satya Jaiswal, wearing a hazy mirror-like light crystal saree, and fresh make-up, sitting in her drawing room. He had walked to Connaught Place from his small room on Ajmal Khan Road. He had paused on the corner of Regal Cinema and had three glasses of 'cold water from a machine', one after the other. Then lighting a cigarette, he had stopped, enticed by the air-conditioned air coming out of Regal's veranda. Then suddenly he remembered Mrs Jaiswal, just like that gust of cold air. Raja Mansingh Road isn't that far from here. In the burning afternoon sunlight, places nearby seem far away. But not for Kapoor. He stops on Regal's veranda and takes three–four puffs of the cigarette. Faraway places drag themselves closer. In front of him lies Henry Moore's reclining woman. An absolutely unformed rock breaks away from a steep mountain and keeps rolling down and drowns in the sea surrounding the mountain. It floats up, then drowns again. Henry Moore's reclining woman. *Reclining Figure.* Kapoor had decided that he would paint a portrait of Mrs Satya. Not today, ten years later. Dr Jaiswal was telling Kapoor how he must showcase the chronological history of Indian folk dances and theatre in his sketches. Museums had to be visited. Huge books of history and archeology had to be examined. So many things had to be done. Uff, not many days remain! The President has agreed to inaugurate the exhibition. The date cannot be postponed any more. 'Kapoor-sahib, whatever art-vart has to be done, you have to do it,' Dr Jaiswal was saying, sitting at his tea table and correcting the copy submitted by one of his writers. The drawing room was quite big, and in the other corner, resting her head on the arm of the sofa, Mrs Jaiswal lay with her eyes closed. Rabindra Sangeet was playing on the radio— When light recedes, you will come. You will come but before your arrival, I will leave with the light. Then you will come when light recedes and I will leave as the shadow of light.

Kapoor had decided that, if not today, in ten years he will make a painting. He can't do anything more than that to erase the darkness of his mind. He could have done something earlier. But at that time, he wasn't obligated to present to Dr Jaiswal the puppet made from bamboo slivers, baked clay and dyed, torn silk fabric that he had named so affectionately: *Glass Fairy*. Dr Jaiswal stared intently at the puppet for some time, then exclaimed happily, 'This is a puppet from Madhya Pradesh. Just 50–60 years ago, they were used in travelling-theatre-type plays. Kapoor-sahib, this is not a puppeteer's puppet. This is a puppet from Madhya Pradesh's tribal theatre. It has historical value!'

Kapoor had placed the puppet on the empty picture stand kept on Dr Jaiswal's study table. It did not have legs, it couldn't stand upright, it would fall . . . 'It has historical value.'

'Kapoor-sahib, you don't understand, if anyone in England had such an old puppet, he would have earned thousands of pounds from an art gallery or a museum. Why are you giving it to me? Give it to an art museum, such a beautiful and old puppet can't be found any more. I have travelled the country many times in search of such a thing,' Dr Jaiswal said, and went to the table to properly fit the puppet to the picture stand.

Feeling somewhat pleased and upset after gifting the puppet, Kapoor had been slowly walking across the lawn of Dr Jaiswal's bungalow when he first saw Mrs Satya Jaiswal sitting in the backseat of a car as long as a ship. The car was slowly gliding along the narrow path of red sand shaped like a bow. Kapoor was tired. Kapoor wanted to run back to

Connaught Place. And drink a cup of hot coffee in an empty restaurant. Glass fairy. Kapoor's glass fairy was lying on Dr Jaiswal's table and smiling. The smile neither widens nor shrinks. The smile is still, like the hands of a stopped clock, still on the white face of the puppet. Kapoor had stopped. The car as long as a ship had stopped too, at the porch. Had Kapoor wanted to turn around and look? But he had moved forward without turning, without looking. On the sides of the lawn, there are long gulmohar trees, their shadows are dense, and Kapoor wants to keep walking under them for a long time. The trees end. A lanky boy, wearing a khaki uniform and resembling a guard, is standing at the main gate. He asks, 'Do you have a matchstick, babuji?' After taking the matchstick and pausing slightly, he looks at Kapoor's face and says, 'There are problems between Sahib and Memsahib. Memsahib has returned, so Sahib will leave now.' And seeing that Kapoor is absolutely uninterested, he says, 'Babuji, I had come for a job. Jobs can't be found? Look at me. First used to ride a scooter. Made a name. Won the speeding contest so many times! Much money, many bottles of liquor! But what can we do about luck? At night, I used to return from India Gate. A boy, a girl with him. Both on the scooter. Said, Not so fast, ride slowly, slowly. In need of air. Take it around India Gate. Take it around on Link Road. I ride very fast. Sometimes, I look back. A boy, a girl, both very beautiful. Both laugh. What can we do about luck! Poor man!'

But Kapoor didn't want to talk with this scooter rider who had now become a guard at Dr Jaiswal's. He put the matchbox back in his pocket. He walked on. He knew that the guard would tell him that he looked back and kept looking back, that the scooter collided with the footpath railing. Accident! That he was taken to the police, and they took away his driving license. It's possible that the guard would tell him that the boy lost his legs in the accident, that the girl became blind; and that he has sworn to never use anything mechanical again. You can't trust a machine, who knows when it might collide with a railing! When it might stop! A machine should never be trusted! Outside the main gate, walking on the side of Raja Mansingh Road, Kapoor was thinking that Mrs Jaiswal must have stepped out of the car and gone into the drawing room, that she must have felt melancholy at the sight of the glass fairy on the table. Beauty should make a person feel melancholy. Kapoor was thinking he would paint a picture. A picture of that melancholy.

But he's had to return to Dr Jaiswal's only after a week. There is a historical exhibition on folk dances and theatre. 'Kapoor-sahib, you have to manage everything related to art and decoration. If you want, hire a couple of assistants. Kapoor-sahib, our country's exquisite and beautiful past, our country's culture, our country's ancient arts . . . we must again know our country and ourselves. Only then true national unity and oneness can be fostered. Then, and only then. Kapoor-sahib, your puppet inspires me . . . Let this exhibition end, these people will certainly send me somewhere as an ambassador, but I will get you some puppetry assignments from the Academy. You will collect samples of all the puppets of the country, ancient puppets! I will get you a good grant from the Culture Ministry, you build a puppet museum, National Puppet Museum! Kapoor-sahib, if we do not protect our national culture, who will?'

Dr Jaiswal was perusing the folk-culture files and examining how much money the government had granted to which discipline, how much more money could be expected and which ministers had agreed to visit the exhibition. Kapoor was silently watching Dr Jaiswal. Dr Jaiswal is around 50 but looks like Oscar Wilde's Dorian Grey. Very handsome and energetic. There is no crease, no laziness, no strife in his manner of talking, smiling, walking, taking out cigarettes from Gold Flake packets and lighting them one after the other! Like a mirror, Dr Jaiswal's personality is shining like a mirror placed in sunlight. Distinct rays of all seven colours are emanating from it. Kapoor feels inferior. Who is he? A commercial artist, who has turned his constraints into his life's destiny. Money is a man's first and last constraint. Money and all that is found in exchange for money. But he reassures himself that a day will come when he, like Dr Jaiswal, will be above money. After that, he will live his own life, a life of art and culture. Then Kapoor starts smiling at the hollowness of his words. Art! Culture! Creation! Expression! Beauty! How pointless and futile these words have become! But then, what possesses meaning after all? Money? An evening with a woman? Falling ill? Going mad? Committing suicide after writing a letter to friends? What is truth? What is sin? What is man himself? Morality? The point of life? The point of creation! What is man himself? Why doesn't he die? Then, again, Kapoor starts smiling at the emptiness of his questions. These questions arise in his mind only when he is tired, or morose, or in search of a friend whom he can verbally abuse and then with whom he can roam in the evening like a vagabond through New Delhi's streets that seem as vulnerable as an estranged woman.

The guard used to a drive a scooter earlier at Dr Jaiswal's. Then he got into an accident. Kapoor moved forward before he could finish his story. Just in front of him, India Gate's mihrab can be seen. It's not so hot any more. Perhaps it might rain by the evening. It must not even be five yet. If he took the scooter, Ravi could be found in his office. It's important to tell Ravi that Dr Jaiswal has given him work. If not much, he will at least get 2000. It was Ravi who had introduced him to Dr Jaiswal from the Folk Culture Academy. He wants to save about 100 rupees and buy a nice camera. Photography helps commercial art very much. Shoot photographs. Then—at leisure—use them as 'models'. Everything seen does not remain etched in the mind like a photograph. A camera is required. A camera is needed for Mrs Jaiswal's picture. Kapoor will tell Ravi. And ask if he has a picture of Henry Moore's great sculpture. *A Reclining Figure*. The reclining woman is an unformed rock, breaking away from a mountain and falling down.

But when he went to Ravi's office and then both of them walked out, went towards Connaught Place, drowned in sweat and scum, and sat inside a small tea shop, Kapoor didn't say anything about Mrs Jaiswal. Ravi asked, 'Dr Jaiswal is impressed with you. Don't miss this opportunity. He will certainly get you placed somewhere. Doctor-sahib himself has lakhs of rupees. And Kapoor, have you met Mrs Jaiswal yet? Be careful with that Royal Bengal Tigress . . . '

Ravi started laughing. Kapoor found Ravi's uncensored laugh terrifying and disgusting. Why does Ravi want to shatter the image being built in his mind about Mrs Satya, Royal Bengal Tigress? A woman reclining on the sofa with her head resting on its arm! Her foggy mirror-like clothes. Green-blue contours of a dusky body! As if fine layers of fog were being laid everywhere. The drawing room was quite long. On this side, Dr Jaiswal was sitting, and far away on that corner, Mrs Jaiswal was listening to Rabindra Sangeet with her eyes closed. All the windows were shut. The sounds of the world outside remained outside. The room was as peaceful and melancholy as a hill station drowned in snow! The magical net of melancholy, coolness and fog snapped. Dr Jaiswal's glimmering eyes refused to recognize him at first. Then he said, 'What do you want?' He had come inside from the brightness of the outdoors and everything in the room looked hazy to him. He was standing, staring. He was saying, 'Memsahib called for the car. The car is outside. Memsahib will go out. Ramsingh said to me, "Tell Memsahib." I have come to tell. The car is ready. Memsahib called for the car.' Saying this much, the boy, feeling anxious, went outside. After he left, Dr Jaiswal smiled. With warm eyes, he looked at Mrs Satya once, with a very wide smile, a very sweet scent spread within his soul. What a sweet and simple woman! The car had gone for a check-up that day. Satya was not a snob like other society women. She'd left on a scooter. Alone! Sometimes in the evening, one really feels like being outside alone. One feels like sitting alone, faraway in a corner of the Children's Park and watching the children running, playing. But the scooter boy got into an accident. Satya had so many troubles that day. Going to the police station, getting the boy admitted to a hospital, arranging for medicines, it was only by the grace of god that Satya wasn't hurt; a poor boy walking on the footpath had been injured. A boy from the university. That boy was never seen again. He never came to our house after the case. Satya had invited him. We would have helped him a little. We could have given him 100–200 rupees. Maybe he had pride. Remained silent. He would have certainly come otherwise! After all, the accident happened because of the scooter on which Satya was sitting. That scooter boy is now a servant here. He is of no other use, he keeps sitting near the gate! At least he can be useful. Anyway, the boy is not bad . . . seems all right . . .

Dr Jaiswal was looking at his wife and thinking such things. Kapoor didn't have the courage to also keep looking at Mrs Jaiswal and finish his image. Kapoor is not courageous. He is not a coward either, but wants to keep his distance from some things. There is a group of new and experimental artists here, every evening they get together in a small studio. Drink neat coffee. Argue. Lie on the floor after taking off their bush shirts and undershirts. And make paintings now and then. A filthy painting of an old woman. Unemployed men standing in cinema queues. A little girl holding in her eyes the old age and black experiences of the world. Spots of dark colours. Kapoor had visited the studio once with a friend. In the middle of the room, an immensely dark woman sat on a stool. She must live in a dirty slum. Must be ill. Must be dead. Empty beer bottles lay around, and artists, surrounding the woman, were painting. Who knows why but that scene reminded him of Calcutta's brothels. He trembled. He felt he would fall ill. That woman's illnesses would enter his breath and he would die. Kapoor is not courageous but he had said, 'This is not art, this is horror! Wouldn't art survive without this woman?

Without this woman? Without any woman? How much money was paid to bring this woman here? Would that money be mentioned in your paintings? Could you do it? You wouldn't be able to, sahib, no one can. Painting doesn't need models, it needs life, real and solid life.'

Real and solid life is different and unrelated to a scooter accident and a beautiful speech on national culture by Dr Jaiswal. A person's life is divided into pieces. There is no one person. There are many people inside one person. Many contradictory situations. Nymphs from Kalidasa's heaven. Constantly warring gods and demons. Times future, past, present. Life is not at one place, which can be presented by tethering it to a mirror, a painting or a poem. Life is every-where. In every moment, in every piece, in everything there is life. And it solely depends on the one who lives the life whether a moment is accepted under a certain circumstance and accepted until when.

Kapoor had returned from the studio after calling those artists horrifying. He had decided that he would make a painting of Mrs Satya Jaiswal. He had already made it. He had made it from the scooter boy's eyes, and from Dr Jaiswal's endlessly happy and endlessly content looks. But Mrs Jaiswal had said, 'Why do you like the colour blue so much? Everything has its own distinct colour.'

And Kapoor, melancholy, had started thinking about colours. It is because of a single colour among thousands of colours that a person gets an important post. Creates large amounts of money. Then one day, bored of monotony, he advertises in a newspaper that he needs a steno girl. He, meaning his office. There are many girls who come for the interview, they do not know typing, shorthand, but they are girls. They are girls who, if they were placed in the show window of a large Connaught Place shop, then people walking along the footpath will stop and say cravingly, 'This plaster model must have been made by some Italian artist.' That man keeps such a girl in his office. Then keeps her in his house. Then marries her. All the other colours are erased, and only monotony's single colour remains—a bright colour. Thinking about colours, Kapoor decides that Mrs Jaiswal wears brightly coloured clothes, wears earrings of white pearls, and yet her colour is blue, only blueness. Such a deep blueness that it engulfs everything of the sky and earth in its dense fog. Kapoor begins painting anew.

It is now evening. A girl is roaming alone in a cemetery. There are graves everywhere. Rows of white stone crosses. Sleeping here is Mrs Martha Graham, who has left with a family's entire happiness. May God offer peace to her soul and reassure her that a few people will never forget her. After reading the epitaph on the grave, the girl wants to return. But she cannot. A man emerges from behind a big grave and asks, 'Are you Martha Graham's daughter? Is your name Satya Graham?' That girl, Satya Graham, sits in the shade of her mother's grave and starts to sob. She keeps sobbing, she keeps feeling scared, she keeps sobbing, and the man who emerged from behind an unknown grave keeps smoking a cigarette besides her.

It is now night. A girl is roaming alone in a large restaurant. There are crowds everywhere. The crowd of any month's first Sunday. She cannot find an empty table. She is roaming through the large hall of the restaurant. She is alone. She is morose. She is also hungry. A man is sitting at a table and drinking cona coffee. He smiles and looks at the girl with a casual glance. Then says, 'I will leave after drinking the coffee. If you want, you can sit here.' Tired and bored of the crowds, the girl sits. The man says, 'If you don't mind, can I order something for you? Coffee? What else? Hot dog? Hamburger? Whatever you want . . . ' They smile at each other. Dr Jaiswal says, 'This is how it happens. People meet suddenly. They spend a couple of moment together. They go off on their own ways.' And, the very next day, Dr Jaiswal advertises for a steno girl in the newspaper.

It is now morning. Kapoor, sitting in the small room on Ajmal Khan Road, keeps thinking about Martha Graham's daughter, Mrs Satya Jaiswal. He orders tea from the nearby tea stall on the footpath. Keeps thinking. What is the point of painting? To paint reality? But it is only the external form of reality that exists in colours, lines, dimensions. Internal colours remain hidden inside. And could the internal be portrayed with colours and lines?

Mrs Jaiswal hates the colour blue. Now, how to portray this hatred in her painting? That evening, Mrs Jaiswal had suddenly fallen silent while laughing. She felt morose. Perhaps she was crying inside. No one cries like that over a film star's death. Kapoor is not interested in films, and he doesn't talk about things he has no interest in. But he saw that as soon as Marilyn Monroe's name was mentioned, Mrs Satya fell silent. Looked morose.

Dr Jaiswal, by then, had drowned in his work. There are files, and on the table, files upon more files. Letters, telegrams, answered telegrams. Dr Jaiswal is considered a specialist of folk art and folk culture. There are many books published under his name. He gives speeches at universities. He doesn't have the time to mourn Marilyn Monroe's suicide. Mrs Jaiswal has the time. Time and mental space. Mental space and privileges. A couple of tears freeze on the corner of her eyelashes. In a choked voice, she says, 'Monroe has left. She took sleeping pills and fell asleep. She didn't wake up again. Kapoor-sahib, have you read Krishna Sobti's novel *Separated from the Stem*? There is a woman who is a flower, and after being separated from its stem, she spends her whole life wandering from place to place. Wandering. She can't stay any-where. No one lets her stay. That is how my girlfriend Marilyn Monroe was.'

Dr Jaiswal returns from the world of files. The Education Ministry has granted three lakhs to Dr Jaiswal's academy. Finally, one important thing is done. But Satya would say that grant won't be given. A high official was displeased. Perhaps he was displeased with Satya. Then how would he be pleased? These officers behave like old kings. Instantly angered. At least, the job is done. Three lakh rupees. The academy should have its own library. A book on the history of theatre should be published. This Kapoor is a good boy. Something must be done for him. Dr Jaiswal comes to the tea table and says,

'Look, Satya, don't think about such things. You will have a nervous breakdown. If you fall ill now, we will be in a lot of trouble. There is a big event. You have to take care of the reception. Let go of Monroe-Vonroe. Right now, Indian culture is more important . . . No, Kapoor-sahib?'

Real pearl studs on the ear. The same white silk saree. That same washed-bright blouse. But where is Martha Graham's daughter Satya Graham? Where has she arrived? Where is she lost? Kapoor picks up the big wall-painting brush and scatters stains of blue on the entire canvas. Stains, big and small. And he smiles like a stupid boy at his own actions. What has he done? What happened to the brightness? What happened to the eyes drowned in love? Intoxication? Terror? Scooter collision? The girl fainting on her mother's grave?

Kapoor came out to his room's veranda. There is a tea stall on the footpath. He calls to the tea seller, 'Send tea for me and send the boy with five packets of Charminar cigarette. Hurry up. I'm working.' And returns. He turns once and looks at the girl standing in the next veranda, who always stares like that, never speaks. She only stares, and if caught, she blushes and goes back inside. Kapoor smiled at her, then returned to his room. He placed one foot on a small stool and then kept standing, looking at the canvas on the easel. Many things started to emerge in his soul. It was Ravi who had introduced him to Dr Jaiswal, and it was he who had turned her off of Mrs Jaiswal. Then he remembered his father. Father has been teaching economics in the same college for the past thirty years. He comes back home from college and drinks in his bedroom. When he is too drunk, he calls Kapoor or his stepmother and starts insulting them, 'My life has been destroyed because of all of you. Money is needed to keep you all alive. And a job is needed for money. You think I feel like working this job? No, I feel like shooting all of them. Now no one reads. Everyone just wants to pass the exams with the help of guide books.' One day, there was no alcohol in the house. There was no money either. Father had started crying like a starved child. That night, Kapoor had run away and come to Delhi. After Delhi, Calcutta. Art School. Modern Art College. Nandalal Bose. Jamini Roy. Chintamani Kar. Then, commercial art. Commercial art is needed to keep living. It's important to draw cartoons. Important to make folders and dust covers. Kapoor returned to Delhi. He became friends with Ravi. He got acquainted with many people. The story started to move forward. The story stopped near Dr Jaiswal. Kapoor stopped.

Ravi opened the door and entered. Said, 'You didn't come to my office yesterday. I should have been angry, but it is you who are sulking. What are you doing?' Kapoor kept standing in the same manner, one foot on the stool, and said in a serious tone, 'Why did you call Mrs Jaiswal a Royal Bengal Tiger? What is it about her?' Ravi laughed. Sitting on the mattress placed in a corner, he said, 'Buddy, not tiger—tigress! Whatever it is, a pitiable woman. A magnificent woman.' Kapoor was looking at the scattered stains on the canvas. Do these stains have faces or not? Or, are these stains mere symbols? Symbols of horror! Kapoor-sahib, come sometime to the hotel where there is a large swimming pool, and where Mrs Satya Jaiswal comes every evening for a swim. Kapoor-sahib, sometime visit the bungalow of that high official who is under Dr Jaiswal's thumb! Kapoor-sahib, at ten every night, Dr Jaiswal returns home and, like Anna Karenina's husband, roams alone through the verandas and rooms and balconies. But why did Mrs Satya start crying over Marilyn Monroe's name? Why did she start to cry?

The boy from the tea stall has returned with packets of cigarettes, and it seems he is the younger brother of that scooter boy. The same frail dying face. The same sick eyes. What would it be like if these eyes were placed on Satya Jaiswal's face? Kapoor smiles. Ravi laughs. The two friends start drinking tea, sitting on chairs across from each other. Ravi said, 'I used to tell you, no, don't get involved with Mrs Jaiswal. Just a few days ago, she collided with a boy on a scooter. The boy didn't die, but he's gone mad. Now it seems it won't be long before you go mad. Buddy, leave all this! Do your job, make money, drink a bottle of beer and fall asleep! That's all!'

At Ravi's words, Kapoor suddenly remembered something Mrs Jaiswal had said. Moving the glass of beer towards him, she had said, 'No, I don't drink. I don't drink anything beyond tea and coffee. Not even champagne! I don't like being even mildly intoxicated. I like seeing and feeling everything with clear eyes and in the right mind. I am a simple woman, Kapoor-sahib! Earlier I was Christian, so I used to call Christ my saviour. Now, after marrying your doctor-sahib, I am Hindu . . . I even go to temples, listen to Mirabai's devotional songs on the radio . . . '

Kapoor had brought over his painting. It was the first time he was visiting at a time when Dr Jaiswal was away at the office. He had spent a lot of money on framing the canvas, a white frame. And Kapoor was elated today. His painting was complete. He felt he had rendered Mrs Jaiswal immortal in this painting. The servant had seated him in the drawing room and gone inside to tell Memsahib. After almost an hour, Mrs Jaiswal came down. She said, 'I was sleeping. You've had to wait a long time. Don't take it otherwise! Women have to make themselves presentable before meeting men.'

Really, Mrs Jaiswal looked presentable that day. She wore no make-up, she seemed very washed and clean, pure! Kapoor picked up the painting wrapped in packing paper and went to the table. And slowly, taking the paper off, he placed the painting right in front of his glass fairy. The puppet was now hidden by the canvas, and Mrs Jaiswal had almost screamed, 'It is a great painting, Kapoor-sahib! It is a great thing!' And she got off the sofa and came near Kapoor. Her own painting had her under a spell. Kapoor was looking at her and trying to understand her reaction. But after standing close to the painting for a minute, she returned to the sofa. Sat there with her eyes closed. Thinking of something.

The servant brought three–four bottles of beer and glasses. Mrs Jaiswal said, 'I don't drink. You go ahead . . . I used to think that you are only a commercial artist. But your painting is a great work of art, Kapoor-sahib! Tell me, what is the price?' Kapoor, holding the glass of beer, kept listening to Mrs Jaiswal. He didn't feel like saying anything. He just wanted to look at her silently. At times he felt like looking at his painting, and at times he felt like looking at the model, Satya Jaiswal. Satya Jaiswal or Satya Graham, it was the same. Satya Jaiswal or any other woman in the world who has been separated from the stem and is wandering. She has stopped somewhere, yet she is wandering.

Ravi finished his cup of tea and said, 'Let's go, Kapoor. Today I'll go with you to Dr Jaiswal's. I have some work with him.' When the two friends reached Dr Jaiswal's, it was almost evening. Doctor-sahib was sitting in the drawing room, looking at the *Life* magazine files. An article had been published about Indian sculptural arts which mentioned him. Seeing Kapoor and Ravi together, he said, 'I was thinking that Ravi had gone off somewhere. Where have you been, all these days? And Kapoor-sahib, why didn't you come yesterday? We were waiting for you. There was a small party here last night. A minister had come. We could have introduced you to him. He saw your painting. He was very pleased. Satya praised you a lot in front of him. She said, "Kapoor-sahib will go beyond Gujral and Hussain." If you were here, you could have met him. Anyway, it's almost certain that your job is done. If Satya makes even one phone call, you will be granted some or the other governmental scholarship to live in Paris for a few years.'

Kapoor turned his eyes towards the table. The painting was gone. Only the glass fairy stood there, silently. Made from white clay, the puppet glass fairy. Kapoor asked, 'Have you moved the painting? It was right here, on the table.'

Entering the drawing room, Satya Jaiswal said, 'Kapoor-sahib, I have gifted your painting to Minister-sahib. He liked my painting, and if the painting is in his house, he will constantly remember both you and me. No?'

Kapoor sat on the sofa without another word. He didn't say anything. He didn't have anything left to say.

PYRAMID

When Rasiklal knocked on the door of his house, Kummi, standing behind him, hardened like a stone . . . Who knows why Rasiklal has brought her here, maybe there is no one at home. Only a servant, who will open the door and fetch a bottle of soda from the crossing.

Kummi's name could have been Kumud, Kumudini, Kamini, Kumari, Kumkum, anything. But all those who know her call her Kummi and offer her a chair or a stool, something, to sit on beside them. She turns heavy and fat when she sits beside people. She feels that she is. She is not lost in a crowd. People know her. It gives them pleasure to know her.

By herself, Kummi is not sad. She feels pleasure. But not with strangers. Not in any house or lane that she has not visited before. She feels scared knocking on the doors of strangers and strange houses . . . A snake might emerge from a man, from within a house might emerge a Royal Bengal tiger that hasn't eaten for 13 whole days. But there was no choice. She couldn't refuse. Rasiklal had said, 'You have to come to my house. My house is in Anandbagh Lane.' Kummi had trembled. She didn't say anything. But she agreed to go.

She has to go wherever Rasiklal asks her to go. This is fate, it cannot be resisted even if one uses the entire force of one's legs and warm hands.

Rasiklal was banging the door latch and the sound was echoing through the neighbourhood—*khan khan, khat khat, khataak, khan-khan-khan!* . . . The evening was not yet over, but at this far end of the lane: silence, darkness, and the distant sound of someone reading the Ramayana—

Supanakha ravana kai bahini
Dusta hrdaya daruna jasa ahini

Pancabati so gai eka bara
Dekhi bikala bhai jugala kumara

Shurpanakha, Ravana's sister,
Wicked at heart, serpent-like.

To Panchavati she once went,
Fell smitten at the sight of two princes.

Kummi asked Rasiklal, 'Is there no one at home?' Rasiklal got angry: 'If there is no one at home, why is it locked from the inside?'

Muniyan opened the door. She was Rasiklal's maid. She came to work every morning and evening. As he entered, Rasiklal said, 'How strange! I have been banging on the door for so long! Have you people gone deaf? Is the mistress asleep? Tell her to make two cups of tea.'

That there could exist such a beautiful room in this lane, Kummi could never have imagined. It's not a room, it's a 'drawing room'! In the faint blue light, everything seems misted over . . . three or four pictures on the wall, pictures of nude women and animals in simple frames, deer in a row with their antlers raised high, naked, unconscious, sleeping women on the raised footpaths of big cities, a lioness drinking from the river . . . animals and women, and animals!

In one corner on the study table is a lamp fixed against the neck of a Habshi woman, along with the last three or four days' worth of mail. Rasiklal hasn't been able to look at anything for the last three or four days because of Kummi. It takes time to lay out the chess pieces, to lay the great trap in the river, and one has to be mindful of the weather. Rasiklal, like a clever and seasoned hunter, waited three or four days for the right weather and then finally, meeting Kummi, said to her, 'I never cheat in a game! But why should I tolerate if someone else cheats! Today you have come to me, which means that this game belongs to me, I have won this game, like King Duryodhan won Draupadi in a game! . . . Come to my house, Kummi!'

Rasiklal lowered the curtain covering the door to the courtyard and said to Kummi, 'Make yourself comfortable. This is my house . . . you can consider it your own . . . If not the entire house, at least this room is mine.' Kummi sat down on the edge of the sofa. She started looking at the books inside the glass-fronted cupboard on the wall.

In the middle of the room is a round table with an ashtray and a vase . . . Kummi plucks out an artificial rosebud from the vase, and lifts it to her nose to smell.

Parting the curtains, Rasiklal's younger brother—Babu—came into the drawing room. It was obvious he had woken up from an unripened sleep. At the very latest, it must have been around eight. But he had been asleep. He starts feeling sleepy as soon as it is around seven. He sleeps after his meal. Even if he's not sleepy, he pretends to be. He doesn't like talking with his sister-in-law. He goes to sleep.

'You go to sleep so early? How will you pass your exams? . . . Go, do your work! Why are you here?' Rasiklal admonished his younger brother studying for his BA.

Babu had just woken up. He was surprised. Big brother never returns home so early. Always well after midnight, sometimes on a rickshaw, sometimes in a friend's car! . . . So who is this woman? And why is she here at this hour?

Babu didn't express any curiosity. Rubbing his eyes, he said, 'Bhabi is asking for matches . . . she wants to light the stove.' Handing him the matchbox, Rasiklal followed Babu behind the curtain. He will change his clothes in the room next door . . . Kummi was left sitting on the sofa, the rosebud pressed to her breast.

Meanwhile, every time the curtain parted, Kummi attempted to gauge the situation behind it. The courtyard is large, a floor of unbaked bricks. Neither the courtyard nor its walls are plastered with cement. There are many banana and papaya trees. On the veranda, casks and canisters are scattered, haphazardly . . . a pile of soiled clothes on the clotheslines . . . a broken perambulator . . . dirty plates, dirty glasses, leftovers . . .

This drawing room is completely different from the rest of the two-roomed house. Different and incongruous! This is a big officer's opulent drawing room. The rest of the two rooms must belong to a third-class clerk, Kummi speculated, looking at the state of the courtyard and veranda.

'Your eyes are closing. Go . . . now, you sleep, Babu! Has Sheena gone to sleep? And Dabbu? Malkin . . . is Dabbu sleeping?' Rasiklal was standing near the drinking-water tap in the courtyard. He was washing up. Neither Babu nor Malkin-madam (Rasiklal's wife, Jaimala) answered.

By now, Jaimala had been informed by Muniyan and Babu that a girl has come home with Rasiklal . . . dark and ugly, but young . . . sitting in the drawing room. Babu couldn't understand why she'd come. Rasiklal rarely brings visitors home. He spends most of his time outside the house, busy with his many occupations, in his office! Once he leaves in the morning, he won't return before eleven–twelve at night . . . But today he has returned so early, with a woman. Who is this woman?

Malkin-madam was in the kitchen, boiling tea. For the past many days, she'd wanted to tell Rasiklal that the pain in her stomach has returned. But there had been no time. Today he has returned early and brought a high-flying item with him! Madam suffers from gas. She feels OK for a month, then ill for four months! But she does all the household chores herself. She is stern by nature, quick to anger. This problem started after Dabbu's birth. Her stomach problem has ripened . . . Rasiklal spends most of his time outside.

Jaimala said, 'If you drink tea now, when will you eat?'
Rasiklal shut off the tap. Drying his face with the towel on his
shoulder, he went towards the drawing room. Muniyan was
standing on the veranda, Dabbu in her arms! 'Babu is sleeping? . . . What are you doing here? You've still not gone home?
Are you staying tonight?' Rasiklal asked, went up to her,
stopped. Muniyan carefully settled Dabbu in her arms and
said, 'Dabbu had fallen asleep before peeing! He would have
soiled the bed. So I brought him here . . . I will put him to
sleep after he pees.' Then she moved closer to Rasiklal and
said softly, 'Malik . . . there is something . . . I need money . . .
not a lot, just 5 rupees! It's very important.'

Muniyan stood there, unable to manage the four-year-old
Dabbu in her arms. Rasiklal started laughing. 'Come, let me
introduce Dabbu to his new aunt,' he said, stretching out his
arms. Muniyan whispered her request again.

'Wait for an hour,' Rasiklal said faintly, pressing her wrist.

Dabbu started crying. His sleep had been disturbed . . .
Rasiklal entered the drawing room, drying his face. Kummi
was sitting as before. Hands folded, knees bent . . . silent and
morose!

'This is my house . . . I live in this house.' Rasiklal smiled.
Kummi began smiling. It pleases him to keep referring to his
own house, his own well-decorated drawing room. His wife
is making tea for him in the kitchen. In the next room, his
maid is putting his young child to sleep. His six-year-old
daughter has fallen asleep on his bed. His brother has gone to
sleep . . . This is his house, his wife is the mistress of the house.

Kummi kept smiling, but she was feeling angry inside. She wanted to return to her own home by nine tonight at any cost. Kummi asked, 'How much rent do you pay for the house? Your neighbourhood is dirty but this room . . . '

'I pay a full 100 rupees,' Rasiklal said spiritedly, putting his hand on Kummi's back. He was wearing a Moon-brand lungi. Lungi and white kurta. And he looked older than his age . . . A triangular moon has appeared on his head, dark circles under his eyes. Perhaps, he is exhausted . . . Kummi felt Rasiklal's hand pause on her left shoulder. She didn't object. She kept feeling Rasiklal's hand.

After talking about his house, Rasiklal started telling her how whenever the maid wanted more money, a little extra over and above her salary, she would ask at this time of the day. She doesn't tell the mistress. And he quoted the colloquial quip, 'If, after dark, a young woman asks for even an airplane, she should not be refused.' And he started laughing, a *kik-kik-kik-kik* laugh.

She understood Rasiklal's quip. Understanding, Kummi turned and held Rasiklal's left hand. Then she said sweetly, 'Please allow me to take your leave soon.'

After some time, Muniyan entered with a tray of tea. Hot steam wafted from the teacups. Kummi liked the aroma of the freshly boiled tea leaves. She picked up a cup and handed it to Rasiklal. She took the other cup and began to drink the tea. Rasiklal said, 'This is Muniyan! She is not a maid—she is the daughter of the house! . . . Her mother used to work here earlier.'

Muniyan saw that Rasiklal was standing close, almost stuck to the woman's back. Malkin, standing behind the curtain, also noticed . . . Malkin went back inside. Muniyan is in dire need of money. Who knows when this woman will leave and when Rasiklal will place a green 5-rupee note in her open hand . . .

There are three women and, without knowing each other, they complement each other. There are three women and they complete each other . . . Malkin hadn't wanted Muniyan to work here. Her mother was here, everything was fine. But the old woman of 35–36 now has a stall selling tea and ghughni-papad at the corner of the Bhikhna Mountain crossing. She doesn't let Muniyan sit at the stall. She says, 'The girl has got engaged . . . she is someone else's thing now. If she sits at the stall . . . and for some reason gets tainted, we will have to listen to her man's abuses.' This is why Muniyan cleans Rasiklal's house . . . The wife doesn't like her ways. The wife doesn't like her. But it's impossible to find a woman who will work so hard and so devotedly for so little money.

Babu was lying on the floor of his room, his eyes closed, after rolling out the mattress and the blanket. Big brother has told him to sleep, so he has to. The sound of someone reading the Ramayana can still be heard from the next house, Muniyan tiptoed into the room and sat by his head. 'Bhaiya-ji, bhaiya-ji, are you already asleep?' Babu opened his eyes. His naked feet jutted out of the woollen blanket. Muniyan was dying to tell him about what was happening in the drawing room . . . She said, 'That woman . . . that woman . . . that woman is sitting stuck to big brother. Both of them are drinking tea . . . Who is that woman?'

'You go home, Munni! If you sit here with me, Bhabhi will get angry. What do I know about who that woman is! . . . Whoever she is, what is it to us? . . . You go, Munni, if Brother overhears us, he will scold us both.' Babu turned over and went to sleep. Not really sleeping, pretending to be asleep. If an educated young woman is laughing freely next to you, if a man is clinging to her and tickling her . . . how can one sleep? Besides, it's not bedtime yet.

Malkin came into the room. She wanted Muniyan to go into the drawing room to ask Rasiklal when he would have dinner. But Muniyan won't go. Malik will get angry if she goes. Babu, his eyes closed, started to snore. 'Why don't you go back home? Has Malik asked you to stay?' Jaimala asked. Muniyan didn't answer. Just shook her head in such a way that it could mean anything.

Rasiklal calls his wife 'Malkin'. He doesn't take her name even when he's angry. Jaimala came to this house 15–16 years ago. After the first night itself, she was called 'Malkin', she doesn't want to go anywhere. She is not a Malkin. Her life is worse than a maid's. A life of hell, Jaimala thinks whenever she is called 'Malkin'. She is unable to do anything beyond thinking and worrying about her stomach problems.

Her two children play outside all day. Sheena is six but has still not started her A–B–C . . . Many home tutors have been hired but they never stayed for longer than four or six days. Sheena reveals her ways on the first day itself . . . Jaimala says, 'Master-babu, if you use physical punishment, our daughter won't study!' Sheena doesn't study . . . Babu wants to study but those two eviler-than-evil children and their village yokel of a mother . . . but he is not allowed to study in the drawing room.

. . . Babu always longs to write poetry-prose by the light of the Habshi-woman table lamp in the drawing room. But even the children do not enter that room. They're scared. They have understood that it's wrong to enter the drawing room. Babu's poems have been published in a couple of special issues of *Magadh News*. He has written one poem on his bhabhi. But he won't get it published anywhere. If big brother hears it, he will know.

Black smoke from the kitchen,
A reclining cat on the veranda . . .
Sick house,
Constant shadows of death
On sick doors . . .
It seems that since centuries a woman
Is standing in the middle of the courtyard,
Silent!

Rasiklal was showing his new album to Kummi. There are no nice photos in the album. Photos of dirty and vulgar women . . . sick men . . . cripples . . . lame, amputated people doing exercise . . . but Kummi didn't hesitate. She kept looking interestedly at the pictures, laughing.

Rasiklal had placed the album in her lap. Turning each leaf, he was introducing and explaining the pictures to her one by one.

In one picture, Jaimala is lying naked on a mat, breastfeeding her infant child. A naked, ugly, vulgar, sick woman—

Jaimala! Rasiklal said, 'This is my wife! I have spent 20 long years of my life with her . . . 5 years of love, 15 years of marriage. See how Malkin's waist has grown so much? Are you seeing? . . . She just wouldn't agree to have her photograph taken . . . but I had to take it. So I did.'

Malkin has shut her eyes in anger. To save her honour! But well . . . can honour be saved by closing one's eyes?

Right at that moment, Jaimala entered the drawing room. She saw the album on Kummi's lap and her photograph . . . she was about to pounce like an eagle to snatch the album away from Kummi . . . then she stopped. She became transfixed.

'What is it? . . . Have you come to take away the teacups? Has Muniyan left . . . or not? Send her to me,' Rasiklal said, without moving an inch from his place. Jaimala picked up the teacups, pulled back the curtain and left the room, looking at Kummi from the corner of her eyes. She placed the teacups on the platform near the tap. The moon was hanging in the sky like a crescent necklace. Banana leaves were swaying in the breeze. The Ramayana recital had stopped in the house next door . . . From the courtyard, she heard Kummi saying to Rasiklal, 'A woman's life is ruined when she gets married.'

'Not the woman's. Her man's. I have been ruined. Malkin lives comfortably . . . What problems does she have?' Rasiklal said, closing the album. Then, after placing it on the table, he held Kummi's face in his hands and tried to kiss her. But he changed his mind while moving his face towards her lips . . . Instead, he stood up and yawned, his arms outstretched.

Kummi, alias Kumudini alias Kumari, feeling shy, turned her face away and stared in the other direction . . . In the next room, Muniyan and Babu were whispering to each other. Jaimala was standing in the courtyard and trying to remove her crescent necklace. She was reminded of removing the necklace after seeing the moon. A blister has sprouted underneath. It will ripen in two days. After it ripens, it will burst. The blister hurts under the weight of the necklace. But the necklace won't come off! The necklace is tight because now there is a lot of flesh on her neck, flesh that's been growing around the neck for the past 15 years . . . Since her wedding, she has not removed this thick gold crescent necklace.

'Someday, I will let you take about 10–20 pictures of me here in your drawing room. It's very beautiful, your drawing room! Have you taken all these pictures? . . . Where did you purchase this bookcase from?' Kummi said, crossing her legs. Rasiklal was pulling a book out of the bookcase. He turned around and said, 'I have made every single thing in this drawing room myself, except for the sofa set! Pictures, vase, the wall bookcase, straw chairs, I have made everything. The rest of the two rooms, kitchen, courtyard, veranda are kept according to Malkin's wishes . . . dirty, disgusting, mud spattered . . . where one doesn't feel like standing even for a minute! The children have grown up but they still don't use the toilet. (No one has taught them yet) . . . they just squat over the courtyard drain! Malkin is Malkin, after all . . . she doesn't pay attention to these small household details.'

Rasiklal pulled out a book from the bookcase. He went up to Kummi. He placed the book in her hands and said, 'I am not a writer. But I had written this book in 1951. A film was made on it that same year . . . Take it and do read it!' On the cover, a woman in the Mulgaonkar style, plump and healthy, fair and smooth skinned, was lying against a bolster, in a classical waiting pose. Above her was written—'*Every Home's Honour: Love-Crazed* by Rasiklal "Lover", BA'.

The young woman kept turning the book in her hands, and Rasiklal kept watching to see her reaction to it. She had none. She kept the book on the table. Then she checked the time on her local Sujata wrist watch. Then she said, 'Now I'll leave . . . I will take the book with me. My work will be done tomorrow, no?'

'Certainly. But not now . . . wait a bit. Leave after 10 minutes,' Rasiklal said like a college boy, in a tone low and soft and trembling with passion . . . Kummi stopped. She was not in a hurry. No one gets upset if she gets home late at night . . . no one. There is no mother, no brother. Her father is there but not there. Kummi often gets back home late . . . She stayed. Rasiklal sat down next to her. Then taking her left palm into his hands, caressing it, he said, 'I know how to read palms! . . . Especially artists' palms! . . . You are the best female artists in the art world.'

About half an hour passed in reading palms' and feet (whether these feet would ever visit foreign lands). During this time, Kummi kept laughing at everything . . . so much so that she started coughing, her eyes began to water and she had to clasp her stomach with her hands.

Then Kummi said, 'I want to go to the bathroom.' Rasiklal didn't want to take her inside the house but he had to. Kummi crossed the courtyard and went into the bathroom . . . the stench stung her nose. She felt she was going to faint. Right in front of her nose, someone had written on the wall with a red–green pencil—'Don't forget to pour water in the toilet after use.'

Rasiklal went to the next room to check on Muniyan. The room's light was switched off. In one corner on the floor, Malkin, the maid and Babu were sitting next to each other on a mat, ear-to-ear, as still as statues of stone!

' . . . she has gone to wash her hands,' Jaimala was saying. She went silent as soon as she saw Rasiklal. But she kept sitting in the same manner, clinging to Babu and Muniyan. Rasiklal said, 'Now arrange for dinner.'

Kummi, coming out of the bathroom, was walking towards the drawing room. Rasiklal came out of the room and said, 'Kummi, won't you have dinner?'

'Not tonight! Some other time . . . ' Kummi went into the drawing room. Rasiklal went with her, to drop her off at the crossing. She sat on the rickshaw and said, 'You are very ill mannered.' And she started laughing. There was no shame or coyness in her laugh but no nakedness either. Kummi's laugh was blooming like a rose on her innocent face. Rasiklal smiled and said, 'One degree less than you.'

Kummi left. Rasiklal took a packet of Capstan and a matchbox on credit from the nearby shop and returned home. He must give Muniyan 5 rupees. And he must complete

Kummi's work tomorrow or the day after. Kummi . . .
Muniyan . . . Malkin . . . Walking back at 10–11 at night from
the Bhikhna Mountain crossing to his Anandbagh Lane house,
Rasiklal kept building a pyramid with these three names, a
pyramid of three playing cards. In the game of Flash, this
pyramid is called a trail. A trail of playing-card wives! . . .
Kummi the queen of hearts, Muniyan the queen of spades,
and the queen of diamonds Jaimala, the mistress of this house!

Rasiklal felt that he was imprisoned inside this pyramid,
like the mummy of an ancient Egyptian pharaoh. He is lying
inside a black ebony coffin, like a mummy . . . Rasiklal
shivered. The queen of hearts, the queen of spades, the queen
of diamonds—he broke down the pyramid and shuffled the 3
playing cards with the remaining 49, and returned home with
swift steps.

The drawing room was open. Muniyan was clinging to
the door. When Rasiklal entered, she said, 'It's getting very late,
Malik! . . . If you can spare the money!'

Rasiklal asked, 'What d'you mean you're getting late? . . .
Your house is just next door.' Muniyan kept standing, her
head bowed. Rasiklal spread himself comfortably on the sofa.
In his mind, he kept thinking about his magical personality.
Really, Rasiklal is a magician! . . . He knows the magic of liv-
ing life.

But just at that moment, as Rasiklal lay on the sofa and
felt his body swelling, slowly turning as light as a balloon . . .
Jaimala entered the drawing room. Hands on her hips, she
stood in the middle of the room. Silently, turned to stone!

Muniyan was sitting on the floor against the sofa, cracking the joints of Rasiklal's toes. Seeing Malkin, she stood up nervously. Two minutes ago, she had told Malkin she was going home. Malkin had seen her off to the door. But after standing in the lane for a bit, she had returned and hidden at the door, waiting for Rasiklal . . . She needs that money right now.

But on seeing Malkin, she stood up nervously and with her head lowered, left the room. Rasiklal kept lying there, his eyes closed, smoking a cigarette . . . Jaimala bolted the drawing room door from inside. Then she went up to Rasiklal and said, 'Come, dinner is served.'

TRACES OF BOOTS ON TONGUE

I have not been to the Greenwood hotel for the past two–three months. It was just that I was feeling quite morose that day and so Shashi said, 'Go out for a while. You'll feel better.' There was money in my pocket, I was excited, I took a taxi to Greenwood. Greenwood is an important pilgrimage of Calcutta nights. On Greenwood's staircases, doors, overhangs, verandas and walls, nymphs stand as they do at Khajuraho, Ajanta, Ellora, Jagannathpuri. They make the carnal apparent in their gestures. The only difference is that those nymphs are not alive, they are mere statues and stone images while these nymphs are alive, possessing body and life.

I was reminded of John Steinbeck, William Saroyan, William Faulkner and other such old and new writers and their old and new novels. I remembered all the girls of *East of Eden* who really lived in brothels and thought their bodies their capital, like farmers thought their farms and workers thought their hammers. I am reminded of the many girls scattered, sprawled and extinguished in novels and stories, in dark-tainted Manhattan alleys, in the hotels and bars of Honolulu, New York and Washington. And seeing these girls enraged me. These girls are Emile Zola's. These girls are Balzac's and Maupassant's, these girls are Tolstoy's,

Doestoevsky's, Gorky's, Kuprin's, these girls are Manto's, mine, ours—

These girls. In one gulp, I drank up a transparent glass of beer and the girls started bothering me. I started to hate the economic system that sculpts such girls, that fertilizes and grows and sprouts such girls.

But then I began to laugh at my own anger. I raised my face from the beer glass and lit a cigarette and smiled, and during that smile, I forgot these girls. I remembered my Shashi. My wife, who places a 10-rupee note in my pocket and sends me off to roam about so that I can cure my headache, or when I return late at night, who even gets angry.

I like Shashi's anger. I like her sleepy eyes, her tired limbs, her moody conversations. If Shashi stopped getting angry with me, my life would perhaps become quite heavy. Because Shashi's eyes are not beastly like Sophia Loren's. Her body is not plump like Marilyn Monroe's, she doesn't know how to flick her hair and speak in a seductive voice, with slanted eyes and pursed lips. She doesn't possess a maddening beauty or hypnotic gestures, because she is a wife, an Indian wife, who can cook, fan and massage tired feet but cannot say that she loves me a lot, with an amorous expression on her face, with warm breath, flared nostrils, widened shoulders and ruffled saree.

This is why no song can be written on Shashi, no story can be written, no novel can be composed, and hasn't yet been composed. For the post of the heroine in a composition, one needs an alien Radha, a Sita kidnapped by Ravana or a modern lady filled with many repressions, perversions and suppressed desires.

This is why Shashi's memory alongside a glass of beer seemed rather senseless and impractical, and I started looking around. The hall had filled by now and a friend of mine was sitting at the corner table. C. F. Kant.

Kant is a new friend. One day, at Indian Coffee House, I was telling made-up adventures of hypnotism and planchette to my friends, like the time I hypnotized Mr Bhatia's wife and asked her which club she visits after 11 p.m. and when I summoned George Bernard Shaw and did a fabulous interview with him and how I . . .

It was then that a South Indian man sitting alone at the table next to mine suddenly asked me, 'Are you a novelist?'

Later I learnt that Mr C. F. Kant was a publicity officer for a Bengali film company and the famous actress Vaasanti Devi was his neighbour. Since then, Kant has become a friend and we run into each other sometimes.

Kant-sahib brought his bottle of rum and glass over to my table and said, while sitting down, 'Hey . . . why are you drinking beer, boy? Bring the bottle here, let me make you a rum–beer cocktail.'

'No, Kant-sahib,' I objected. But Kant-sahib doesn't understand objections. He drew the two bottles close, winked and smiled. The smile gave a polish to his ebony face. Another reason for the polish was because an Anglo-Burmese girl had just passed him, wearing a backless blouse. Knowingly or unknowingly, Kant-sahib stuck out his foot slightly, which made her stumble. She turned around and looked at the owner of the foot. She first got angry, then smiled, then walked away after making her body a little more poetic.

'All the girls who come to this bar are tramps.' I said seriously, like some moralist philosopher.

'My dear Kamal-babu . . . if you find one decent girl here, I'll get the City Father to give you a doctorate in . . . sociology . . . yeah . . . understand?' Kant-sahib answered while mixing the alcohol from bottles into glasses. The hall was thick with cigarette smoke, a cocktail of alcoholic scents, a song playing on the radiogram.

Who who who who who who will give me a penny
Who who who
My name is Sweety Sweety Jenny
Who who who
Come to me when the night is dark and rainy . . .
Who who who

Howls of laughter and voices filled the room. The backless blouse had settled at an empty table far away and was drinking Coca-Cola.

At first, I didn't notice. The second time, I didn't understand. The third time I understood that the girl, or that woman, or that woman dressed as a girl, was sticking out her tongue to Kant from behind the Coca-Cola bottle. Kant was already watching her. Even so, I brought it to his notice, 'Why is she showing you her tongue?'

'No idea.' Kant said without paying any attention to what I had said, because he was absorbed in watching her crimson lips against her white teeth, and the repetitive motion of her tongue going in and out of her mouth. But the whole thing didn't last long. A big and robust-looking Navy boy sat down at the table of the woman with the tongue. Kant became morose and said, 'Let's go, Kamal-babu. There's nothing to do here. The dance will begin at eleven. If we must, we'll come then. Let's go now. We'll roam outside . . . '

We paid the bill at the counter and walked out on to the street.

At the Chowringhee Road and Bhowanipore junction, a young genteel girl was standing near the bus stand. She had three or four, fat and slim books in her hands and her eyes were filled with exhaustion, indifference, helplessness. I merely saw her face, because I don't like looking at anything else. I don't like it because I am a religious man, and our religion doesn't allow us to drown ourselves in beauty. So, I merely saw her face. On her face were withered white lips, the whole cosmos could have existed in their expanse. She had small eyes, at their corners were lines of kohl resembling coal-tarred roads down which one could reach a nondescript dak bungalow. Kant-sahib said, 'Just wait here! I'll be back with a cigarette.'

I stopped. The kohl roads saw me and the lips widened. I started drowning in them like a ship with a broken mast. This sense of drowning embarrassed me. I was just about to blush when a long and thin tongue came out of the genteel girl's white lips, brandished like a snake outside its burrow, then went back inside. It was clear that the snake wanted to come towards me. I didn't quite grasp whether the gesture was pure or dirty because I belong to that hilly area in Dehradun district where girls don't show their tongues. They only show that without which nothing can be done.

I quickly crossed the footpath and went to the cigarette stall where Kant-maharaja was arguing that 2 annas was equivalent to 13 new paise and not 12.

Walking along again, when I told Kant-sahib about that genteel girl, he started laughing. Then he patted my back and said, 'Yaar Kamal, why are you up in the hills! You don't understand this little thing? Even now, in so many countries, people don't shake hands, don't say tata-bye-bye, they just show their tongues. Have you studied animals? Have you seen a cow? How it loves its calf. It licks the calf with its tongue. To show tongue is a manner of showing love, no? You don't know?'

I didn't answer. The mixed effect of beer and rum was trying to enslave me. Till Basusree Cinema, Kant kept lecturing about love, about love being a difficult art and that there was no better expression of love than with a tongue.

Suddenly, at the start of a small alley, he stopped, lit a cigarette and said, 'Bhai-jaan, my place is here. Thanks, the evening passed nicely. See you some other time . . . OK. Tata.' And without waiting for a reply, he turned into his alley, as if he had remembered something important.

I walked on alone. Kalighat arrived. I felt like going towards the temple and seeing the fine details of Bengali terracotta architecture. I felt like studying the busy devotees and the group of beggars chasing them. I felt like standing in front of Mother Kali's idol, about whom a popular Hindi poet had written, 'Mother Kali's tongue seems to be made of pure gold.' I felt like it, but Mother Kali's tongue reminded me of the Anglo-Burmese girl's tongue in Greenwood, the tongue of the genteel Bengali girl standing at the bus stand and I felt scared.

I was scared and, standing silently on the veranda of a cinema, I started looking at the poster of the film *Ami–Tumi–Bhalobasha*. A 12–13-year-old girl was also looking at the poster and feeling embarrassed at the sight of the reclined actress on it. Her embarrassment almost stopped when she noticed me standing close to her. She raised her face and started staring at me, innocently.

Fearing the expansion of her lips and the appearance of a snake from between them, I quickly left. Now the effect of the alcohol was decreasing. The weight of my head was increasing. I climbed up the stairs and reached the second storey of the cinema. There is a famous restaurant here where there are more girls than boys. I didn't want to be among girls but I wanted to have coffee, my head was spinning. It felt like my head had exploded.

I lit a cigarette when my coffee arrived and started thinking about the point of the tongue, what's the advantage, what is the use? The tongue is used for speaking, eating, breaking a loose tooth, scaring children, for example Kalighat's Mother Kali. But here the tongue is being used for something else altogether. The tongue has turned into a messenger . . . in the Mahabharata era, milkmaids were Radha's messengers, now Radha's tongues have turned into Radha's messengers.

Two young women were sitting at the table in front. Both were of the same age, wearing sarees of the same colour, blouses of the same colour, they seemed like sisters. I felt they were both simultaneously sticking out their tongues at me. As if I were a doctor and boils had sprouted on their tongues.

Far away in the corner, a woman of 30–32 was sitting with 2–3 boys and eating Mughlai parantha. At first it seemed like her lips were dry and she was wetting them with her tongue, but then I had to stop looking.

Behind me was a married couple. There was a boy of about three in the husband's lap. There was a sense of peace in the wife's eyes and seeing her I too felt at peace. I kept looking for a long time at how the father was feeding tea to the boy with a spoon. I kept looking for a long time, then the wife smiled, and, out of the husband's sight, started looking me in the eye and touching the tip of her nose with her tongue. When I saw this, she extended her round face a little, blushed and pursed her lips, then started waving her tongue at me.

It was as if I'd gone mad. The tongue of the married mother seemed to me larger than the thousand-headed serpent's tongue that had been used to bind the Sumeru mountain during the Churning of the Ocean.

I took the last sip of coffee, emptied the cup and started waiting for the waiter. It was just then that I saw Mr C. F. Kant entering with a South Indian girl. The girl was a wearing an expensive Karola-style saree with a deep yellow blouse, and a thick braid of pearl flowers in her bun. The girl was about 14–15 at most, and her body was expressing that it was made to dance the Kathak or the Bharatnatyam.

Kant-maharaja was standing at the door, talking to the waiter about something important; the girl kept walking forward. When she saw me staring at her like an idiot, she felt proud of her shapely body and shrugged her shoulders slightly so that the corner of the saree fell to the ground. She bent over to pick it up, our eyes met, and in a manner courteous and civilized, she stuck out her almost beautiful tongue at me.

Then Kant-sahib saw me and, walking towards me, he screamed, 'Hullo Kamal-babu . . . you came to this place too?'

Sitting at my table and straightening the chair for the girl accompanying him, he said 'Wow! We meet again! Wow. Sit, Saroja, sit! This is my friend, Kamal-babu! And this is my sister, Saroja . . . '

Saroja didn't flinch at all at this introduction, didn't blush, spreading her legs and her Karola saree with nonchalance, she took a seat and, cutting her words with alcohol, said, 'It's a pleasure to meet you . . . '

I went mad. I felt as if Sir Kant's sister Saroja was not there. I felt as if the married mother was not there. I felt as if the mother was not there, the wife was not there. There was no one, no one, only a large ocean and night and darkness and tongues bigger than the huge waves at high tide are colliding with my ship and there are many holes in my ship and my liver . . .

I went mad but I did not cut off Saroja's tongue with my pocket knife. I just smiled and said, 'Saroja-sister, it's a pleasure to meet you.' And I kept waiting to see if Saroja would stick her tongue out again.

In the evening, when I returned tired from the office, my head was aching badly. I said to Shashi, 'If you have some money, give it to me. My head is heavy, I had to work really hard today. I think I'll go to the coffee house.'

Shashi, at first, stared at my face carefully for a long time trying to gauge if my head were really aching. Then she said, 'There's no money! In total there is one 10-rupee note and still a week before payday. If you break the note, all the money will be gone in two days. Why waste your time! While you read *Navbharat Times*, I'll make tea. OK?'

I didn't answer. I only smiled at this clever housewife who runs the whole household on just a hundred rupees a month. Shashi saw my smile, stuck her tongue out to mock me, then went outside, laughing. I found Shashi's innocent gesture of sticking out her tongue and then running away very adorable, because I had seen that there was not even a single trace of boots on her tongue.

Notes to the Translation

PAGE 1 | **Ranchi's mental hospital:** Founded in 1918, the Ranchi European Lunatic Asylum (today called the Central Institute of Psychiatry, Ranchi) was the largest psychiatric facility in colonial India during the 1920s and 1930s. It soon acquired notoriety for being a preserve of the deranged. See Waltraud Ernst's *Colonialism and Transnational Psychiatry* (London: Anthem Press, 2013) for a detailed account.

PAGE 2 | Built in the 1930s, **Connaught Place** continues to be a popular commercial and cultural hub in the heart of New Delhi. With its art-deco buildings, upmarket shops and coffee houses, attracting both locals and foreigners, it became a symbol of modernity in post-Independence India.

PAGE 3 | **blue bottle of cona coffee:** Probably a reference to a vacuum brewer used to prepare coffee. United Coffee House, established at Connaught Place in 1942, was known for its cona coffee and affordable snacks. See Bhaswati Bhattacharya's *Much Ado Over Coffee* (New York: Routledge, 2018) for a detailed account.

PAGE 4 | **dry day:** A day on which the sale or public consumption of alcohol is prohibited.

PAGE 15 | At a time when Indian magicians and illusionists were belittled for their lack of sophistication, **P. C. Sorcar**'s mesmerizing performances, flamboyant and audacious in equal measure, became renowned the world over. For more, see John Zubrzycki's article on the magician for the *BBC*: https://bbc.in/2xMUH1g

PAGE **15 | perfect pair:** '*jugal-jodii*' in Hindi. Literally, 'twin siblings', the phrase is commonly used to refer to the pair of deities Radha and Krishna, the paradigmatic couple of Hindu mythology. This kinship phrase is suggestive of the undifferentiated oneness that is at the culmination of pure love.

PAGE **16 | Manmohini:** Literally, 'heart-ravishing', 'captivating'.

PAGE **19 | M. Smiles' book about character:** Probably a reference to Samuel Smiles' 1871 work entitled *Character*. Smiles' international bestseller *Self-Help* (1859) lends its name to the genre some scholars argue its publication established. His books were translated into several Indian languages.

PAGE **21 | Phool-babu:** Literally, 'Darling flower'. Term of endearment.

PAGE **21 | ligatures:** In the Devanagari as well as other scripts derived from the Brahmi, successive consonants lacking a vowel sound in between them are physically joined to form a ligature or a conjunct consonant.

PAGE **21 | Pasis:** A historically marginalized Dalit community in North India. Their name's etymological roots are contested and an example of the politics of caste self-identification. Early orientalists argued that their name derives from the Sanskrit *pashika*, meaning one who uses a noose used to tap toddy wine from a palm tree. While many voices from the community themselves argue that their name derives from the Hindi word *pasina* (sweat), more specifically the sweat of Parshuram, one of the avatars of Lord Vishnu. This is seen as an attempt to self-identify as Kshatriya, a historically dominant caste.

PAGE **21 | Musahars:** One of the most marginalized Dalit communities in North India. Their name, derogatory in origin, is said to be derived from the Bhojpuri *mūs* + *ahar* ('rat eater').

PAGE 23 | **Bhavanand:** Literally, 'fount of joy'.

PAGE 24 | **red loincloth in the style of Hanuman:** A reference to an underclothing worn by men, especially by wrestlers and ascetics, and by the Lord Hanuman in Hindu mythology.

PAGE 24 | **Black mare, crimson reins:** A modification of the Hindi proverb *Buddhii ghodii laal lagaam*, 'Old mare, red reins', meaning an old person trying to dress or act younger than their age.

PAGE 28 | **Ramganjwali:** A woman from Ramganj. In Hindi, the suffix *-wala* / *-wali* denotes identity, as in *chai-wala*, 'one who sells tee'.

PAGE 30 | **Draupadi is helpless . . . Draupadi with swathes of saree from above:** With the advent and spread of the lithographic press *circa* the late-nineteenth century, Indian calendars were rife with illustrations depicting religious scenes from the epics, nationalist icons and, later, movie stars. Combining Indigenous subjects with Western styles and form, Indian calendar art has come to be recognized as a genre in and of itself. For a detailed account, see Yousuf Saeed's *Partitioning Bazaar Art* (London: Seagull Books, 2023).

The typical calendar illustration in this story depicts Draupadi's *vastraharan*, a scene from the 'Dyuta Parva' in the second book of the Mahabharata: Draupadi, the common consort of the five Pandava brothers, is disrobed and humiliated by their cousins the Kaurava brothers, because her 'honour' has been gambled away by Yudhishthira, the eldest of her husbands.

PAGE 41 | **Inter:** Short for Intermediate, a series of standardized tests taken by school students at the end of Grade 12 in India.

PAGE 43 | **Khajuraho statue:** Many of the reliefs and panels that adorn the walls of the Khajuraho temples in Madhya Pradesh depict sexual practices.

PAGE 51 | Bombay's Ahuja affair was also like this, based upon which the film *Such Are the Ways of Love* was made.: In 1959, Naval Commander Kawas Nanavati was accused of killing his wife's lover, Prem Ahuja. The case, which gained nationwide attention, was tried by a jury, and Nanavati was found not guilty of murder. The verdict, however, was later overturned by a higher court, and the case eventually led to the abolition of jury trials in the country. The reference here is to the 1963 Hindi film *Yeh Rastey Hai Pyar Ke*, which dramatized these events.

PAGE 55 | pranayam: Yogic breathing exercises and techniques, believed to augment one's vitality. From the Sanskrit *prana* (life force) + *ayama* (extending).

PAGE 58 | Like Duryodhan . . . save his own life.: A reference to a scene in the Gadayuddha Parva (a subsection of the Shalya Parva) of the Mahabharata, where Duryodhana hid inside the Dwaipayana lake to escape from the Pandavas. When Yudhishthira finally found him, Duryodhana offered the kingdom of Hastinapur as a gift to save his own life. However, Yudhishthira refused it saying that warriors do not accept gifts and offered to Duryodhana that he could fight any one Pandava of his choosing. Duryodhana chose his nemesis Bhima and lost.

PAGE 59 | The Churning of the Ocean (*samudra manthana*) is an important episode in Hindu mythology that recounts the churning of the ocean of milk by the gods (*devas*) to obtain the nectar of immortality (*amrita*). According to some traditions, Airavata, the white four-tusked, seven-trunked elephant of Lord Indra, is said to have emerged from the Churning.

PAGE 59 | *The Seven Year Itch*: The 1955 American film—immortalized by Marilyn Monroe's wind-blown white dress—about a man, married for seven years, resisting the itch to cheat on his neighbour (played by Monroe).

PAGE 65 | *Reclining Female*: Of the 10 or so reclining figures sculpted by Henry Moore before Rajkamal Chaudhary's death in 1967, none has the name 'Reclining Female'. Judging by its description, Chaudhary was probably recalling Moore's *Four-Piece Composition: Reclining Figure* (1934) or his *Reclining Figure 1939*.

PAGE 66 | WARRIORS DON'T WORRY ABOUT THE RIGHT TIME: This story was originally written in Maithili and translated by the author into Hindi with the title unchanged: *Surma Sagun Bichare Na*.

PAGE 66 | Bhurishravas and a pot of venom. But Lakshmi won't emerge.: Hindu mythological stories have numerous local variations, often orally transmitted, with no acknowledged ur-text. This plurality of 'tellings' makes it difficult to decipher allusions such as the one used by Chaudhary here. The author might have been referring to a local Maithili telling of the *samudra manthana* which has no reference in classical texts. For a detailed account of the politics of 'original' and 'variant' texts, see A. K. Ramanujan's 'Three Hundred Ramayanas' in *Many Ramayanas* (Berkeley: University of California Press, 1991).

PAGE 67 | She comes straight from Shiva's planet. From the Kailasa mountain.: In Hindu mythology, Mount Kailash is regarded as the abode of the Lord Shiva (also known as **Mahadev Bholenath**, 'the great lord of innocence'), 'The Destroyer' in trinity of supreme divinity in Hinduism.

PAGE 73 | Sarat Chattopadhyay: Early-twentieth-century Bengali novelist and short-story writer.

PAGE 75 | Rani Rashmoni was a prominent zamindar, philanthropist and social reformer in nineteenth-century Bengal. She patronized several educational and religious institutes and also founded the famous Dakshineswar Kali Temple in 1855.

PAGE 80 | **Buddha and Vaishali's city-bride Ambapali:** In some parts of Ancient India, courtesans excelling in various dance and art forms were given the title of *nagarvadhu*, literally meaning 'bride of the city'. According to the Pali tradition, Ambapali, *nagarvadhu* of the city Vaishali, converted to Buddhism when Gautama Buddha visited the city towards the end of his life.

PAGE 82 | *Yes, desire is important . . . matter of our yearning.*: Translation by Mustansir Dalvi of Faiz Ahmad Faiz's Quatrain 'Na aaj lutf kar itnaa ki kal guzar na sake'. Available online: https://bit.ly/3kSTsH1. Translation © Mustansir Dalvi, 2012.

PAGE 84 | **Amar matha . . . dubao chokher jaley:** A song composed by Rabindranath Tagore in 1906.

PAGE 93 | **SISTERS-IN-LAW:** The original Hindi title, 'Nanad–Bhauji' uses two different kinship terms for 'sister-in-law' impossible to render in English with brevity: **Nanad** refers to one's husband's sister; **Bhauji** refers to one's elder brother's wife.

PAGE 97 | **VENI SANHAR** (literally meaning 'slaughter of a braid') is a Sanskrit play written in the eighth century CE by Bhattanarayana. It is based on an incident in the Mahabharata, where Dushashana forcibly drags Draupadi by her hair to an assembly. Draupadi vows that she will keep her hair untied until she soaks it with Dushasana's blood. At the end of this play, Bhima kills Dushasana, applies his blood to Draupadi's hair and ties it into a braid.

PAGE 110 | **Regal Cinema** was the first cinema to open in Connaught Place in 1932. It closed its doors in 2017.

PAGE 110 | **cold water from a machine:** In the days before packaged drinking water, street carts, with the phrase '*machine ka thanda pani*' painted on them, dotted the main thoroughfares of Indian cities, selling refrigerated water by the glass, as well as other beverages such as fresh-lime soda, to beat the summer heat.

PAGE **121** | **Krishna Sobti's novel** *Separated from the Stem*: Sobti's 1958 Hindi novel *Daar se bichuri* has been translated and published as *Memory's Daughter* (New Delhi: Katha, 2007). The translator has used a more literal translation of the novel's title for the salience the phrase has in the rest of the story.

PAGE **129** | **Ramayana**: A quatrain from the *Ramcharitmanas* (3.17), an epic retelling of the Ramayana by the sixteenth-century poet Tulsidas.

PAGE **130** | **Habshi**: Derived from the Arabic for 'Abyssinia', the derogatory term 'Habshi' refers to people of Southeast African descent living in India, most of whom were brought to the subcontinent through the Arab slave trade. A more acceptable term used to identify the group, 'Siddi' (Arabic for 'my lord'), also possesses connotations of their history.

PAGE **132** | **Malkin**: Literally, 'mistress of the house'.

PAGE **140** | **Mulgaonkar style**: A reference to the style of painting pioneered by the prolific artist Raghuvir Mulgaonkar (1918–1976). An oeuvre which spanned over 30 years and included more than 7,000 paintings, Mulgaonkar depicted figures from Hindu mythology in a corporal, realist style, often resembling contemporary film posters.

PAGE **140** | **Sujata wrist watch**: A reference to the first watch, named Sujata, specially made and marketed for women in India by Hindustan Machine Tools (HMT). HMT started as a machine tools manufacturing company but diversified into watchmaking in 1961. It established India's first wristwatch manufacturing enterprise with a tie-up with Citizen Watch Company of Japan. The watches were named after popular names in India, including Nutan, Rajat, Sona, Sujata, etc. It came to be a symbol of durability and indigenous entrepreneurship in post-Independence India.

PAGE 149 | 2 annas was equivalent to 13 new paise and not 12: An anna was a unit of currency in India equal to a sixteenth of a rupee. In 1957, the Government of India decimalized its currency, sub-dividing a rupee into 100 new paise. Thus, making 1 anna equal to 6.25 new paise, and 2 annas equal to 12.5 paise. However, since one could only trade a whole number of paise, Kant is here arguing that 12.5 paise should be rounded off to 13.

PAGE 149 | Mother Kali's tongue seems to be made of pure gold: A reference to the Kali deity in the Kalighat temple of Kolkata, one of the oldest Kali temples. The deity's tongue in the temple is famously gold plated.

PAGE 151 | Sumeru mountain during the Churning of the Ocean: In many versions of the *samudra manthana*, Mount Mandara is seen as an earthly manifestation of the mythological Mount Sumeru, considered to be the centre of all physical, spiritual and metaphysical universes. Mount Sumeru features as a common motif in Hindu, Jain and Buddhist mythologies. Its representations can be found in stories, folktales, paintings and architecture all across South and Southeast Asia.